So Clever You're Thick

Tales for Well-Dressed Cynics and Optimistic Ragamuffins

Cathleen Davies

4 Horsemen
Publications, Inc.

Published By: 4 Horsemen Publications, Inc.

4 Horsemen Publications, Inc.
PO Box 417
Sylva, NC 28779
4horsemenpublications.com
info@4horsemenpublications.com

Edited by Jen Paquette

Library of Congress Control Number: 2025936684

Paperback ISBN-13: 979-8-8232-0888-8
Hardcover ISBN-13: 979-8-8232-0889-5
Audiobook ISBN-13: 979-8-8232-0891-8
Ebook ISBN-13: 979-8-8232-0890-1

Dedication

For my best friend Thomas. We'll travel the world, and he'll bring the sunshine.

And Dr. Robin, who I always thought was cool.

Acknowledgements

Thank you to Karl, Florence, Rex, and Annie for helping me proofread. If there's any mistakes, blame them and not me.

Thanks 4 Horsemen for continuing to publish my nonsense. It's weird to specialise in genre fiction and erotica and then occasionally big up some mental case in the UK pretending to be a literary genius, but I respect your eclecticism.

Thanks to Sophie Sherman for bringing me cups of tea and coffee, and sometimes little snack boards, when I'm writing. You are the best flatmate a failing writer with a geriatric cat could ask for.

Thanks to the poetry nights in Norwich, especially LPS and Taeside, who is an exceptional talent.

Thanks to all the people who read my work, especially my distant family in the North West who seem to think I'm the next Hemingway.

Previous versions of some of these stories can be found in *Five on the Fifth, Cafe Lit Magazine, Sad Girl's Club, The Wire's Dream, The Anti-Misogyny Club, For Page and Screen,* BDA Publishing's *Your Body My Rage,* and Sparkle and Blink's *Quiet Lightning.* Thank you to all of them who have published my stories. Read small journals, support local artists, go see bands in dive bars with 30 other people, live little, feel loads.

Thank you mostly, and yet again (miraculously, at time of editorial publication, she is still alive), to Fliss the cat.

Contents

Cooked Blue

Call me "hypocrite." I deserve it.

I ask strangers if I can stroke their dogs too often. I delight in unlikely animal friendships. I send so many pictures of my cat to group chats that I sometimes catch winces of embarrassment from the married couples who, for some reason, still deign to associate with me. This, I understand, is who I am.

I like jazz and tea and candles made from beeswax. I like trees of green, red roses too, and watching tiny fishes circle through clear, ocean water. I like sunflowers, bluebells, and snowdrops in spring. I like doing cartwheels on springy, green grass.

When I see videos from inside the slaughter-houses, I feel sick. Snapped chicken necks and pig squeals, cows stumbling backwards, knowing something's amiss but not quite what, their eyelashes so long, so dark. It's enough to make you weep.

Call me "hypocrite." I deserve it, but at least I'm going to try. I roll my shoulders back and smile, imagining clear skin, yogic positions, birds landing on my open palms. I will be clean and new and pure. Who could possibly have cause to complain?

"Christ, does this mean I have to start cooking rabbit food when you come round?"

"Not at all. I understand that sanctimoniousness is one of the biggest drawbacks of veganism, and I won't participate in it. The world is awful and full of fear, and no one should be made to feel guilty for having to eat. Besides, if I'm living on chickpeas at home, I'll probably fancy a steak by the time I get to yours."

"What? So you're not even doing it properly then? Seems like a waste of time."

"Do you want to feed me rabbit food or not?"

"Whatever. Meat is more moral than veg anyway, so…"

"Two cokes?"

"Thank you."

"Yes, thank you. What are you
talking about?"

"I'm talking about how eating vegetables is
more immoral than eating meat."

"No, it isn't. It objectively isn't. Look, I'm
not going to force you into it, but eating
the corpse of a pained and tortured animal
is not morally superior to cauliflower."

"Sorry to bother you again.
How is it you said you'd like
your burger cooked?"

"Rare, please. As bloody as possible."

"You're a pig."

"And extra bacon if it's not too late."

"I'll ask the kitchen."

"An animal."

"I thought you liked animals."

"A shit, then."

"Well, that's not as non-judgemental as you promised a few minutes ago. You're not getting a steak next time you're at mine."

"You're being deliberately provocative."

"I'm not. I'm being Asian."

"What? What does that have to do with anything?"

"My nainai almost died in the Great Leap Forward. They had to eat the family dog. I bet you'd tell them that was evil."

"Of course I wouldn't. Needs must. Anyway, it's the industry I hate, not the principle."

"A-ha!"

"A-what?"

"If you care about humans at all, you shouldn't be vegan."

"And why is that then?"

"Third-world farmers are suffering. Everyone's eating all their vegetables (which, by the way, are imported by massive world-ending, climate-ruining planes), and it means no one in Kenya can get their own avocados. It's bad for biodiversity. I mean, eat vegan if you enjoy it…"

"No one enjoys it."

"… but don't convince yourself you're moral because you're not. In fact. if anything, being a vegan makes you racist."

"Cheese burger rare with extra bacon?"

"Right here."

"And a mushroom burger?"

"Thank you."

"Enjoy your food."

"I will!"

"I won't."

"And just think: you'd have been morally better if you had the forethought to get something delicious."

You know it's worse for you than smoking cigarettes, right? Without the right minerals and vitamins, your body goes into starvation mode and starts to hold onto fat so it's harder to lose weight. And the hormones that you get from dairy are essential; otherwise, the blood will start pooling in your eyeballs and streaming down your cheeks, and you'll die of dehydration in a terrible, anaemic state. It's true. It happened to a mate of mine when he went through his hippy phase. They had to put him on dialysis.

You know that people on vegan diets starve their pets for entertainment? Do you know how misogynistic PETA are? And you're still doing this? That seems pretty hypocritical for a feminist. They kill more animals than they save, you know? And did you know that all the pigs would die out if we didn't farm them? And cows would run amok and stampede the children, and the children would implode under their hooves, and their cries would be heard for the centuries to come?

Do you know plants scream when you pull them from the ground? Do you know they're capable of feeling pain? The reason radish tastes stronger the longer you eat it is because it's releasing stress signals to the rest of the plant to inform it of the impending danger. Did you know that? Do you care? A succulent told me he met you the other day, and you were a real arsehole. Apparently, you interrupted in the middle of a story he was telling, and then everyone got distracted and started listening to you instead, when actually, the succulent was really shy, and it took a lot of guts for him to start telling that story, and you ruined it, you fucking ruined it. How could you?

Don't you know it's too late for the planet anyway? You know the environment changes as the years go by, and yes, it's gradually heating up, but that's normal, and there's nothing we can really do about it? Honestly, it's inevitable, but people are too stupid to realise that, and now they're saying it's too late, but it was always too late. We can't change the planet. We're not that powerful. Isn't that the kind of shit you liberals always say?

I don't feel bad about eating meat anyway because I always eat the whole animal. That's right. I stop by the butcher and get tongues and hooves and eyes to eat. I put them in a soup and marinade them for hours, and by the end, they're so tender that the meat slips down your throat like water. I'll eat anything, me, and I'll kill it if I have to. I'd do it with my bare hands like a hunter/ gatherer. I'll strangle the life out of a baby lamb for fun, the little whores, they love it, and I could wrestle a pig, fuck you, I'll do it, I swear to God, I'll do it. You know I'm not soft like you.

Can't eat meat. Evil.

Can't eat cheese. Same reason.

Can't shop in big supermarkets. Gotta go local.

Can't buy new clothes. Fast fashion. Charity shop only. Only sustainable brands, and nothing that funds the genocide in Palestine. (So, I guess then, to be a good queer/person, it's gotta be Lucy & Yak. Christ alive, I fucking hate Lucy & Yak.)

Can't smoke. Can't drink. Definitely can't do drugs. Drugs are exploitative. They ruin whole communities in South America. So does drinking. So does smoking. We are *all* addicted drones.

Can't buy plastics. Ocean's full of rubbish.

Can't buy anything. Capitalism.

Must buy some things. Help the economy. Eat out to help out.

Go contactless. Save paper. Save the planet. Get change for the homeless. The homeless are struggling. No one carries change anymore. And all these storms and random heat waves... The planet is dying. Save paper.

Buy *The Big Issue.* A good cause. Charity. Don't think about the paper. Would be better as an e-zine. Hand over change. Make conversation. Make them feel human. It's *important* to make people feel human.

Read the news. Stay informed. *The Big Issue:* A good cause.

The new space race takes off

*Branson, Benzos, and Musk: boys
and their overpriced toys*

Glance back at seller. Homeless refugee.

Glance back at planet. Still on fire.

Glance back at meat industry. Who the fuck cares?

Go home. Get a steak. Share it with pet cat.

Be a fucking hypocrite. Hate yourself and hate the world.

Cook steak extra bloody. Imagine it's a billionaire. Snort a line of coke and set something on fire.

Kill everything right now. Condone first-degree murder. Advocate cannibalism. Eat shit. (Quote Divine. Try not to think about how they killed that chicken.)

Kill a fucking chicken.

Pour milk over your naked body as you sob in the foetal position.

Listen to The Smiths on repeat. Kidnap Morrissey and slice off pieces of his flank to feed to your aging cat.

If anyone criticises you, say it's self-care.

Set appropriate boundaries.

Drink more water.

Eat more flesh.

Make sure to save room for the eyeballs, ears, and hooves. They're the best bits, don't you know?

And they taste even nicer when they're

Cold or

Cooked blue.

Declutter

Brian didn't bleed radiators, change oil, or build flatpacks, but John did. John'd always been the practical one, which was funny because everyone assumed he was the "woman" in the relationship, a misconception Brian was happy to reinforce. The realisation that John had left him hit Brian again in the early morning hours when he wrapped his duvet around himself and felt surprised at the lack of resistance. Labeija didn't even bother sleeping on their bed anymore. Instead, she curled up on the living room carpet, one eye on the front door, the other hidden by her floppy ear.

It was easy to see why people *had* thought John was the "woman" despite his skills in practicality. His persona, Miss Teak, was certainly very feminine. John didn't do that bearish drag with a beard beneath blue eyeshadow. He committed to his looks; half his wages went back on wigs and eyelashes, glittering dresses that winked from the rails of their cherished wardrobe, shoes that cost a bloody fortune... But even though he made his money dancing on stage in a frock, he was still the one who'd put up all the furniture. John never left anything to Brian because, deep down, they both knew he couldn't nail two blocks together.

It was for this quite selfless reason, Brian supposed, that John had left most of the furniture behind. Suitcases full of John's things had gone, but the telly stayed, and the telly-stand. The bed was still upright, although it was messier now and cold on one side. Brian wondered if he should feel guilty for sleeping better since John had left. Without anyone stumbling in and turning on the bathroom light, swearing as they washed off the cake-thick makeup and glitter, (Glitter! In six years together, they'd never had a sink free from bloody glitter), Brian finally got a night's sleep with no interruptions. Any other time that might have been a good thing, but when he woke up at 7 a.m., well-rested and slightly hungry, he realised the day wasn't quite as ready for him as he was for it. He'd been so busy sorting out this mess with John that he hadn't had time to go to the shops. It was a Saturday morning, and he didn't have any coffee. The tubs usually lasted such a long time that Brian couldn't remember ever running out before. Course, he couldn't leave the house to get any. The delivery was coming any time between 8 a.m. and 4 p.m., so he had to stay in all bloody day.

The only thing John *had* taken was the wardrobe, and Brian needed to get a new one built. His clothes had been roughly folded in a sad pile on his chair for weeks now, and it was starting to make him depressed. Their old wardrobe was a thing of beauty. Five panels of mirrored, sliding doors, so smooth they never rattled, in all its glossy black glory. What should have been Brian's office had become John's changing room, and soon his desk was streaked with finger swabs of eyeshadow, foundation, and highlighter. John always said that because they worked such different hours, there was no reason they couldn't *both* use the desk, but Brian couldn't stand the clutter. That was one good part of this; at least he'd got his office back.

It was strange that John was so scruffy in his "dressing room" because everywhere else he was immaculate. The house was always spotless, the tea-towels ironed and folded beautifully, shoes stacked neatly on their little rack. A week or so after John had left, Brian'd gone barefoot into the kitchen to make himself a (weak, supplies were dwindling even then) coffee and realised that all these *bits* were stuck to his feet. Brian hadn't known sweeping up mattered so much. Now he was better with cleaning, but it still wasn't great. Nothing was as sleek and fresh as he liked it, and he couldn't quite put his finger on why, but he knew that when John and his mate had come round to dismantle the wardrobe, he'd been embarrassed to let them in. And God! He'd been in his pants! Not sexy ones either. The baggy ones he slept in with an oversized t-shirt.

He hadn't learnt his lesson, obviously, because when the doorbell rang at 8:15 a.m., he answered in his pants then too.

"Alright mate?" he said to the delivery guy, holding back Labeija with his foot. Brian didn't know why he called everyone "mate" when he first met them or indeed why he felt the need to lower his voice half an octave. He had this ridiculous notion that he had to make himself straight, as if this fat delivery man would run away screaming if he knew he was face-to-face with a homosexual.

"Alright mate, sign here please…"

Brian did so, all the while thinking, *Did he just copy me on purpose? To mock me? Or is "alright, mate" such a universal greeting that repetition shouldn't cause alarm?*

Labeija scarpered off with a disappointed whimper.

The delivery man left the parcel by the door, which was annoying. It was too heavy to carry into the bedroom without struggling, and Brian didn't feel like struggling on a morning without coffee. He lay out the parts on the living room floor and stared at them, perplexed. He'd sprung for the Kleppstad, but looking at it, he wasn't so sure it'd be as simple as the reviews claimed. Five or six big chunks of wood, two doors, handles, hinges, and a thousand little bits and bobs he didn't know what to do with. John had an electric drill, but he'd taken it with him. Everything went up fluidly with that thing. You could tell John enjoyed putting things together in the same way he liked doing crosswords or bejewelling his tights. Brian would offer to assist:

"If you need help with any of the heavy lifting…"

"No!" John would say, holding up a hand. "You'll just get in the way and wind me up. You know you will. If you want to help, stick the kettle on."

John was good like that, to be fair. He worked well with his hands. Brian wished that his parents had met John like that, sweating through his t-shirt while he put together an Ikea bedroom set. They never saw him properly, the way Brian saw him. His family had only met John a handful of times, once at lunch, then the hospital, the funeral, and the last time, at that awful party.

So the "fours" went on the "fives" and had to be screwed in with an Allen key, but they shifted backwards and forwards and were too heavy to properly align. With a couple of screws, Brian managed to get a bit of an L-shape going, and he thought he might take a break now the shops were open, get himself a coffee and some breakfast, but that wasn't going to work because he couldn't stand the clutter, didn't want to walk into his flat with shopping bags and find a scruffy carpet and an L-shape on the floor looking up at him. L for *Loser*. L for *Loveless*. L for *Like you know how to put up a wardrobe, you div*. He decided to do the other side so he could come back to a U.

The first time they'd all met, it'd gone okay. His parents were very old by that point, his mum on her last legs. They didn't want to stay out too long, so it was a pub lunch rather than a weekend visit, and an exhausting three-hour drive each way. John was on the charm offensive. He took Brian's mum by the arm the second she opened the door and walked at her insufferably slow pace to the car.

"Here we are, Mrs Jackson. Your chariot awaits."

Brian wished John wouldn't try so hard. His dad shuffled along last, having taken about ten minutes to lock the door.

The food was good, though. Hard to go wrong with a roast. John pretended he wanted to share a bottle of red with Brian's mum, which was annoying because Brian knew he preferred white and was just trying to people-please.

"Bloody hell, Bri! I'd drink warmed-up vinegar and say it was lovely. It's all the same to me!"

Whatever. They shared out the bottle. His dad had a pint.

"How's business doing?" he asked Brian.

"Fine. Ticking along. Always gets a bit busy this time of year, you know with er…"

"Year's end?"

"Aye, that's it. Feel like I'm never bloody away from it, to be honest."

"He's not wrong," John said. "Every night in the living room, *year's end* this, *year's end* that. I feel like a qualified accountant just listening to it all!"

"Yes, what *do* you do, John?" Brian's mother asked, cutting delicately into her lamb.

"Bar work," Brian answered for him.

John looked offended, but Brian ignored it. He doubted there'd be a scene until his parents were gone, so it was just a matter of biding his time.

"Oh, very social. That'll suit you," Brian's mum said, her eyes twinkling.

"Well, you know me, Vivian. Love a natter over a pint glass."

Small talk was awkward after that. John went quiet so Brian and his parents slipped back into their usual discussion cycle, talking about the food, and the various other Sunday dinners they'd had, who did the best roast potatoes, how his sister was doing, and the kids, and all the other conversation topics that drag on whenever one's forced into a familial environment.

They dropped off his parents with a promise that next time they wouldn't leave it so long. Brian secretly hoped that they would.

In the car on the way home, John was silent. Brian knew it was a pointed silence but was too knackered to talk anyway, so decided to embrace it. John kept sighing, his hands clenched on the wheel, his breath building up until eventually he snapped.

"Bar work?" he asked.

"Well, you do work at a bar, don't you?"

"Oh, yeah. I work at *some* bars, sure. Also some clubs, festivals, charity events…"

"Alright, Miss Teak, I get the point. You don't *just* do bar work."

"I *don't* do bar work. I do drag. That means I'm a performer, a designer, a make-up artist, a beautician, a singer, a dancer, a comedian, a bloody activist half the time, so the next time I meet your parents, can you please refrain from calling me a bar-man?"

That was another thing about John's practicality: he was good with a list.

"And what exactly is wrong with being a bar-man?"

"Oh, don't give me that nonsense. This isn't about class. This is about the fact you're too pansy to admit who I am and, by extension, to admit who *you* are."

It was quiet then. Brian felt tired. His mum was in her seventies now, and she looked thinner. She couldn't walk unassisted anymore. There was another stent being put in her leg in March, but no one knew how she'd get on with the surgery.

"Sorry," Brian said, sighing. "No, really, I am sorry. I shouldn't have said it."

"Bar work," John scoffed, but Brian knew he was softening because he added, "What about when they come to ours next Christmas, ey? Your dad asks for a Tom Collins, and I give him a bloody Sex on the bloody Beach, what then?"

Brian laughed.

"He only drinks lager. I think you'll be fine."

But next Christmas never came. First it was Covid. No one had any of the vaccinations then, and they couldn't take the risk. Then it was Brian's sister's turn to host because she wanted a big one with the whole family, but that was too far for them to travel, so they gave it a miss, and then Brian's mum died. They'd known it was coming. There'd been a fall. They moved her from ward to ward while she wilted like an old bouquet. Brian and John went up to visit once, but she was out of it. John sat beside her, holding her hand as he babbled on and on saying stuff that didn't make much sense.

"Oh, Viv, you would not believe the journey we've had. Traffic all the way down. Roadworks on the M1. I mean, honestly, they pick the worst times to start with all that rubbish. Well, maybe it's not the worst time for *them,* but it always manages to be the worst time for *me.* How are you keeping anyway, love? You look well, doesn't she, Bri? Little paler than last time, but you need to tell me your diet plan because your cheekbones are divine!"

Brian just sat there, looking at her. She already seemed dead, looking like a Halloween decoration with her patchy hair and pale skin. There were blue spots on her face he'd never seen before. He had to keep reminding himself that this body was his mother.

The hinges weren't attaching to the wardrobe door, and Brian wondered if it might be socially acceptable (perhaps even high-fashion?) to have an open-plan wardrobe, a design with a back, sides, and rail but with his glorious selection of black trousers, trackies, and work shirts on display. The back had been the fun bit. He just had to hammer it in place *whack, whack, whack,* tiny, little nails going all around the edges.

John had been good with funerals too. Some people are. He had stories about Brian's mum. God knows how when they'd only met twice, once when she was unconscious, once when he'd been too pissed off to talk. Still, he went on about her sparkling eyes, her stunning bone-structure, her kind spirit, her brilliant sense of humour. He asked questions about what she was like as a little girl and talked loudly to deaf relatives. Brian's great-auntie seemed delightedly baffled by this loud, overtly charming character, and asked him who he was and what he did.

"I'm Brian's friend," John answered. "I do bar work."

Brian had never loved him more.

That night, they'd tried to fuck. Well, Brian had tried anyhow. He'd said they had a hotel room, and how often did that happen? Couldn't waste the opportunity, could they? John smiled and kissed him hard on the lips. Then he stopped. He put his chin on Brian's shoulder and took a deep breath.

"The drive was knackering, babe. Can we just sleep tonight?"

It was only when Brian felt suddenly and completely relieved that he realised this was exactly what he wanted.

The good news was that the doors were on. The bad news was that Brian had smashed the mirror in the process. The doors were stiff and didn't shut properly, so he thought maybe it would be easier to do with it standing up. *Now, how am I going to get this upright by myself?* he thought. Well, he gave it a go, didn't he? Tipped it over in the process. Smash. Seven years bad luck, they say.

Brian's 50th had been a big one, even though he didn't want it to be.

"We need this," his sister had said on the phone. "Craig and I will drive Dad and the kids down. You just stay there and relax."

"I don't know, Stace."

"Bri, it's been a shit year. Dad barely leaves the house now; I'm worried he'll go next. Anyway, turning 50 is a big deal! We can book a nice restaurant, have some drinks and dancing. It'll be a nice trip for us. And it'll cheer everyone up."

"Can't we do a big thing for *your* birthday instead?" Brian asked.

"Ah yeah, the big Five Four in April next year. That'll be a showstopper. Come on, Bri!"

"I've got too much work on to plan a party. You know that."

"I'll plan it!" she said. "I'll get John to help. It'll be fine."

And help John did. Every time Brian walked into a room, there'd be a dramatic exclamation.

"Do NOT look at my screen! It's a surprise!"

Brian sighed. "John, please don't make this too big. You know I don't like all that glitz and glam."

"Darling, do you think we met yesterday? I know exactly what it is you like, and I plan to deliver. Low-key, classy but not fancy, and *cazh-you-al*. You'll love it, I promise."

It was a Saturday night at the function room of the Toad & Swan, a lovely sit-down meal with three courses, none of them too pretentious, a bottle of wine plonked down every few seats, smart-casual dress, one long table, banners, balloons, and cake. Lemon cheesecake to be exact, a bizarre choice for a birthday, but Brian's favourite, as John well knew. Brian smiled. John was right. It was exactly the kind of thing he liked. Ironic that he'd put so much effort in because, in the end, he couldn't even go.

"I cannot FUCKING believe it," Brian heard him shout from beneath his laptop a few days before. "They've booked me at *Velvet* this Saturday. I told them I needed this weekend off. They've already started advertising!"

"Ah well," Brian said. "These things happen."

"Well, I'm not doing it. It's their fault. I told them I needed it off, and it's their fuck up. Sod 'em," John rallied, but Brian could tell by the way he was biting his nails that he didn't mean it. *Velvet* was a great club. They always got John the best gigs, and if he refused to show, they probably wouldn't book him again. Brian placed a hand on his knee.

"I'm going to ask you a favour, as your loving partner. Please go to work and earn us lots of money instead of sitting down for a boring dinner with my family."

"It's not going to be boring. Are you forgetting I planned it?"

"Please go to work instead of sitting down to an enjoyable dinner with my family."

"*Exquisite* dinner, I think you mean. I could go to the dinner for a bit and then rush off. I won't be on 'til about midnight."

"Darling, it takes you hours to get ready, and you wouldn't be allowed to have a drink. You'd be stressed out the whole time."

There was a long pause.

"Are you really sure you don't mind?"

"Not in the slightest. You can use all your tips to spoil me."

And that night, they did fuck, passionately, at least in part because Brian was relieved. He liked to keep his family and relationship as separate as possible, but John made that hard by being so bloody affable.

The dinner really was exquisite, though. Tomato soup and crusty bread, a roast dinner with excessive amounts of gravy and wine. Lots of wine. Stacy was on top form. Even his dad was laughing again. John had invited Brian's mates from the office, which was a pleasant surprise, especially since he'd managed to only invite the ones that Brian was fond of. Never before in his life had Brian received so many gifts. The table was heaving with bags, baskets and bottles, wrapped up carelessly in cellophane. Good ol' John. Brian reckoned he must have stipulated the gift part of the invitation quite heavily.

Brian was just starting to feel good, slightly drunk and ready to enjoy the attention he usually despised, when it started:

"This song goes out to a very special birthday boy. We love you, baby." It was John's voice, but he'd gone all whispery and strange. A moment later, Brian saw why. John turned the corner with a microphone. Or rather *she* did, Miss Teak, in full Monroe get-up. The white dress clung to his padding and revealed the top halves of plastic breasts. A mole was painted delicately on his matted face, and the wig was waved just beautifully into soft, blonde curls.

"Happy birthday," he sang raspingly, "to-a you-ooh."

Brian's stomach dropped. This was a nightmare. Why would John do this? In front of his dad. In front of his *workmates*. It was everything Brian hated. Typical of John, he had to make it all about himself.

"Happy Birthday... Mr. President..."

Miss Teak seated herself on Brian's lap, pouting at him. Brian heard them all laughing. He pictured his dad's face, shocked, confused. His nieces and nephews had their phones out to record. His coworkers were there; this would be watercooler talk.

"Happy Birthday… to-oooh you-oooh." After a breathy finish, Miss Teak leant in for a kiss. Brian couldn't stand it. He stood up and left, forcing John off his lap in the process. He felt sick and angry, but he wanted John to follow him so that they could come up with a plan to save it, to make it go back to normal again. Could he go home and change, maybe? Could they pretend it was funny, like something from a stag-do? Impossible. No stag-do prank had such beautiful contouring.

Outside, he waited for John to join him, but John didn't come. He finished his set while Brian sat down, panting. As the anxiety attack began to pass, Brian started to wonder what was taking so long. The music was still going. He heard the cheers and whoops.

"My darlings, my darlings, I can't thank you enough."

And then finally, out he came. Maybe he saw Brian sat there, maybe he didn't; either way he kept going, stilettos clicking on the corridor floor.

"John?" Brian called after him. "John, where are you going?" He turned a corner and Brian followed him. "John, can you talk to me please? Where are you going?"

"I'm going home, Bri," John said, and Brian was surprised to hear his voice breaking. Why would *he* be upset? This was all his doing.

"What, to change? Are you coming back or going to *Velvet*?"

"There was *never* a gig at *Velvet*, Jesus Brian. How blind can you be? I wanted to surprise you. I thought after six years you'd be happy to see your partner. Obviously not."

He stomped out of the carpark and waited on the street, pulling his phone out of his bra. Again, Brian followed.

"*Now* what are you doing?"

"Ordering a fucking Uber! I had a vodka to steady my nerves. Lot of good that did."

"And then what? Are you coming back or just pissing off? To be honest, I have no idea what just happened. You said you weren't coming, then you turn up in drag, then when I'm embarrassed, which you must have known I would be…"

"Oh, *must* I? Must I have known that? Maybe after six years, it was naïve to expect you'd stop being embarrassed of me. My Uber's here."

"Just wait a minute, hey. Why do you keep saying that—six years?"

"I'm going."

"I need to talk to you."

"Then come! I'm not stopping you! But I can't stay feeling this ridiculous in public."

John got in the car. Brian groaned and slid in next to him. The driver smirked while they confirmed the address. As he started driving, John turned to Brian.

"So, what is it you want to say?"

But Brian was looking at the cabbie's eyes in the rear-view mirror.

"Let's just wait 'til we're at home."

John scoffed, tears rolling down his cheeks as he turned towards the window.

The wardrobe was up, stiff in parts, wobbly in others, but it was functional. Annoying that he'd put it up in the living room and not his bedroom, but that could be resolved. Or maybe he should put it back in the office, where the old one had been. The carpet was still a strangely bright green in that spot, and Brian didn't know whether he should deep clean the carpet or just dirty that one side of the room.

The phone rang and Brian jumped. Labeija looked up excitedly, but Brian waved her down, sighing as he saw the number on screen.

"Hey Dad!" he shouted. His dad had been going deaf for years. "How are you?"

"Oh, fine, fine. How are you?"

"Not bad, yeah, not bad."

"Now, Stacey told me about you and John."

Oh God. Did everyone in his life have to keep sticking their bloody oar in?

"Yeah, don't worry about it, Dad. It's fine."

"Well, your mother's not here to talk about these things anymore so. How are you?"

"Yeah, Dad, I'm fine. It's all fine."

"She said it was something to do with the engagement party…"

"Engagement party? No Dad, it was my birthday party, remember? I turned fifty. You were there."

"I thought it was an engagement party; that's what your sister said."

"No, Dad. It was my birthday."

"Oh. Well, anyway, we wanted to let you know we're here. I'm sure you must be upset."

"Honestly Dad, I'm fine."

"Well, losing your fiancé…"

"Boyfriend."

"… It's hard, you know. I understand it. I know your mum was taken by him."

Brian paused and took a deep breath. For whatever reason, a lump was rising to his throat, which he couldn't understand because this was far kinder than he had any right to expect his geriatric father to be. He gave a shuddering sigh before continuing.

"It's fine. It wasn't all that surprising really."

But of course, that was a lie. It was surprising. Brian hadn't believed it was happening as it happened and was amazed at how quickly his feelings changed from angry to terrified.

John had been sitting on the small kitchen chair. His makeup had smudged from the tears. Brian thought it should have looked hysterical, like a cartoon clown, but actually, it didn't look like that at all. John looked like Grace Kelly, even with his wig off and the stocking over his head.

"I can't keep doing this," he said. "I can't love myself when I'm with someone who doesn't love all of me. You keep wanting to change me and I can't. I don't want to. And I'm sick of the shame."

"Is it my fault I don't want to live like a walking cliché?" Brian scoffed.

John shrugged. "Maybe it's not," he said. "I don't know."

That's when Brian had started to panic. He knew it was ending because John wasn't fighting back. He didn't want to stand up for himself, he didn't want to make a scene, and it didn't even matter anymore if he was right. Brian wanted to promise John he'd change, but he didn't know if he could or if he even wanted to. It'd been too long that they'd stuck with this same argument. Brian wasn't sure if he even felt it anymore, but God knows he couldn't let it go. If he accepted John's career now, would he still feel the embarrassment at times, like a phantom limb?

"Never mind," John said, attempting to laugh and then stopping. "Never mind."

"Dad, I've got to go," Brian said. "I've got this furniture to move and I need to run some errands, you know?"

"Oh, alright, alright. Well. You take care of yourself, won't you?"

"Yeah. Sure."

Brian hung up. He still hadn't eaten; he wasn't hungry anymore. Instead, he wanted to sleep for a while. How strange. A good nine hours he'd managed last night, and somehow he was still tired. The living room was fucked. There were nails in the carpet that would be a nightmare to pick up and inevitably end up stuck in Labeija's paw. The wardrobe was far too heavy to budge. He should've done it when it was all in the box. Why had he been so stupid? Why did he insist on doing it himself in the most cack-handed way possible? How did he always manage to mess these things up?

It was roomy when he climbed into the wardrobe. He tried to close the door on himself so it would be completely dark, but his fingers still stuck out a little and a slither of light hit his left shoulder.

Depressive Giant Nightmare Boy

In the sunshine, it was magic. Every morning, before each dreary day, I could at least look forward to the walk. My house was an orange box on a soulless cul-de-sac, right behind the woodlands where light beamed through tree branches like UFO headlights. I'd crunched under the bright, blue sky through snow and rested on the fallen trunks during sweaty summer hikes. I'd loved the bluebells in the springtime and the orange, purple cascades in the autumn; I loved it all, and it was always bathed in sunshine.

On the weekends, I took Millie. I'd begged my parents for Millie half a decade ago, making her fully *my* responsibility when it came to the daily walks, the feeding, the picking up dog-shit. I think my mum thought this would teach me a lesson, that responsibility would be something I'd grow to resent, but I never did. Millie was a good girl, and I loved her; loved her more, in fact, than I might have loved you.

Nothing impressed you. Teachers were boring, and no one taught you anything you wanted to know. You rolled your eyes when George shot Lenny. You didn't even turn up for parents' evening. I knew you weren't there because I spent two hours looking out for you. I wanted to see what you'd wear. I only ever got to see you in our uniform, but Gabs said he'd seen you outside Tesco's once and apparently, your outfit was sublime. You wore fishnets, a crop top, and a leopard-print jacket, unzipped so he could see your skinny stomach and (he said, I don't believe) wiry pubes creeping up towards your belly button. I almost buckled imagining what your legs would look like in those tights. I ached to put my arms around your skinny, naked stomach.

I don't know why you kissed me. No one else gave me a second thought. I had exactly two friends: Sam and Gabs. They played video games and farted on each other's pillows. I always changed my sheets after they'd been round, just in case.

Maybe it was because I was tall and skinny. I don't know how. I ate and ate but never got fat. I slept loads too, but I always felt tired.

Or maybe you kissed me because I played the piano.

"I liked your song," you once told me after Music. "It was cool."

If I was a more honest person, I would've told you I didn't write it. It was just a piece I had to learn for Grade Five, a piece I hated because the ripples were too hard and fiddly. If I was a more honest person, I would've told you that your comment made me want to scream with happiness. Instead, I just nodded and said "Thanks" like girls complimented me all the time. And I don't know. My mum was pretty nice. I had a little sister who worshipped me. Some weird girl with a removable brace had had a crush on me once. I'd just never been complimented by somebody so hard to impress before.

Then there was the time you spoke about me, not to me. I passed by you as you stood with the smokers by the school-gate. Sam and Gabs were arguing about Minecraft, and Sam made that weird, dinosaur noise he does, which always makes me cringe. Jamie, your ex-boyfriend with his ears pierced all the way round, called us freaks and snorted. I never liked Jamie. I was glad when you dumped him. You'd smiled at his remark but then said:

"Curtis is alright."

I didn't even know you knew my name.

I guess that's why I felt bold enough to smile at you when I passed you in the hallway. I guess that's why I could brush my arm against yours in English. I guess that's why, when I found you outside the health-point in your PE kit with an ice-pack on your head, I didn't just keep walking.

You'd gotten a concussion from PE when that tough old cricket ball had hit you in the head. A lump was forming beneath your black and curly hair, the melting ice dripping down your un-blushed cheek. You were arguing, like always. This time with the nurse.

"She won't come for me. She has work."

"You can't walk home by yourself with a possible concussion. It's dangerous."

"Well, I'm gonna be walking home by myself at 4 anyway, so you might as well just let me go now."

"If your mum hasn't picked you up by then, I'll drive you home myself, but you need to be observed in case you have a fit."

"I'll take her home," I said.

You looked up at me from the green, plastic chair, and after a moment of confusion, you smiled. The health point nurse nodded:

"Alright Curtis, good lad."

If I'd been Jamie, it wouldn't have been allowed. It would've been seen as an excuse to skive, to get out of class and into trouble. But I never spoke up in class, and people knew we couldn't possibly be friends. It seemed gallant and responsible for me to walk you home. She didn't even question why I wasn't in class myself. The truth was, I'd heard about your head in Science, and nothing could keep me from you when I knew you knew my name and thought I was alright.

You walked with me in silence for the first five minutes.

"How's your head?" I asked.

You smirked. "No complaints."

"That's good. Where do you live?"

"Past Oaktree, on the cul-de-sac."

"Near me then." I nodded. Of course, I'd already known that because I saw you sometimes walking up the pavement, headphones plugged in and smoke trailing behind you while I gawked behind the hedges wondering if it was worth missing out on the woods one morning just to watch you walk to school. The trees always won out in the end. I felt less like a stalker when I chose the trees. "We'll cut through the woods on the way, if you want. It's a little more time but I think it's worth it."

You scoffed.

"Why?"

And suddenly I was embarrassed. "Dunno." I shrugged. "It's nice."

"Okay, woods it is. Whatever."

We were only there five minutes when I knew something was wrong. The trees weren't so together anymore. The ground was slippery, and soggy leaves stuck to the bottom of your combat boots.

"It's usually much nicer than this," I said.

"Whatever. It's still nicer than the roads."

"I walk Millie here. My dog."

"You like dogs?" You smiled and I thought it was mocking until you followed it with, "That's sweet."

And it was easy for you, easy to the point of being offensive, the way you could wrap your arms around me and kiss me on the cheek. Your lips were soft and warm against my dry skin, and you looked beautiful when you smiled at me. You made it easy, so easy, for me to lean down and kiss you on the lips with an open-mouth and clasp the back of your neck, stroking your hair behind your ears, kissing you harder until you flinched.

"Ow."

"Oh God," I said. "Oh God, I'm so sorry."

"No," you said. "It's fine. It's just my bruise, you know? The cricket ball."

"Oh!" I laughed. "Thank God, I thought I was doing something wrong, that maybe you didn't like it, or I was bad, or…"

"Curtis," you asked me, suddenly serious, "was that your first kiss?"

I felt my cheeks go red. "No. Not really. Well, yeah, I guess. I was just saving it for someone special." I paused while I thought of the right word, and I remembered from some desperate corner of my mind the old Oasis song. "Someone electric."

"Oh, for fuck's sake, Curtis!" It wasn't put on anger. I could see that you were livid.

"It's true! I mean it. You're special! You're…"

"Not like other girls?"

"Exactly!"

"Damaged in a cool, tragic way that maybe you can fix, and maybe when you fix me I'll have no choice but to be indebted to you? Or maybe you're the one who's damaged, right? Maybe I can fill in all the gaps that your parents, your friends, your fucking dog can't fill? Maybe I'm magic, special, *electric*, maybe I'm so mature for my age, and maybe, just maybe, I don't actually want to be."

You sat down on the tree stump, the same one I had rested against so many times before, and even though by this point I was certain you were mental, you managed to only look tired.

"My head hurts," you said quietly. "And the other girls laughed when it hit me. And my mum doesn't even work. She just doesn't want to drive five minutes down the road to pick me up because she's shit. And all I wanted was to kiss the nice, tall boy who plays the piano and offered to walk me home. I can't keep doing this. I never asked to be this way. I never wanted to be electric."

It took a lot longer than it should have for me to sit down next to you. Perhaps I should have put my arm around you, but I didn't. I should have said that I was sorry that the other girls were mean, I was sorry your head hurt, I was sorry someone saying you were special was enough to make you feel so sad and scared. Instead, I just said: "Sorry," and then a little later, after we'd been quiet for the longest time. "It wasn't a bad first kiss as things go. You don't have to love me just because you kissed me. The kiss was good enough."

You lay your bruised head on my shoulder and then, finally and far too late, I put my arm around you.

"Thank you," you said.

The damp leaves fluttered a little, and I wished that I could still see the place as magic, but now I saw it for what it was: a woodland in a built-up suburban area, littered with too many empty beer-cans and the smouldering attempts at campfires. The pollution wouldn't kill these trees, but it wouldn't make them happy either. We sat, and for a short time, things were just about fine.

"You know you play piano?" you said, looking up at me with big, brown eyes, still shiny from the tears.

"Yeah?"

"Well, if you ever want to write a song about me, don't."

Dirty Stop Outs

I was so used to seeing Toni by then that my heart didn't ache when she walked in. My legs didn't shake, and I didn't stand up awkwardly to greet her. Instead, when she clocked me from across the busy pub, I raised a finger in a slight wave, my head still resting on my hand. I'm not sure if my moderate calmness was because I didn't fancy her anymore, or because I was so used to fancying her that seeing her didn't make that much of a difference. Her lips were thick with filler and glossed over with pink. Fake eyelashes made her look drowsy, and foundation covered her freckles. She wore blazers with shoulder pads now, so she looked like a unit even though I knew she was so small undressed. Apparently, Craig liked this new look. I didn't, but that was probably for the best. If I saw her in an old baggy t-shirt of mine, I'd fall in love all over again.

"I got you a pint," I said.

"Bitch, I'm not drinking! I have cocktails later. I can't show up smelling like *beer*."

I'd forgotten about her affected RuPaul speech now, the *yas queen* bullshit that I'd never heard before when she was legitimately queer. I can't remember her ever having a problem with beer before either.

"Well, it's here now."

She sat down opposite me and sighed. "Just one then."

"Well, don't do me any favours, like." I was being snide, but she wasn't paying attention. Somehow, without me realising, she'd pulled her phone out of her handbag and was already distracted.

"Sorry, hang on," she said, tapping with acrylic nails. Toni was one of those people who was constantly on her phone but never replied to messages. She'd get back to you eventually though, and her response would be so charming you'd forget you were mad in the first place. The last conversation I had with Toni went a bit like this:

Can we talk about this thing with Craig? This "blessing" bullshit? I miss you.

(Seen)

And then three weeks later:

Hey girllllllll, sorry for the late reply. I've been so busy with work. Craig finished moving in last month. I swear to God, I don't know why he has so much stuff. I'm like, what did you bring a kettle for? I told him I didn't need any kitchen stuff, and this doesn't go with ANYTHING else. There is a THEME. I know I'm ridiculous, but I spent so long planning my dream houses that now I've got one, I'm not sacrificing my ***themes***. *There's still boxes everywhere, it's driving me mad!!! I swear when us two used to live together we only had like, one wardrobe between us in that tiny, shitty room and we were absolutely fine. But anyway, I miss you too! It's been too long! How're things going at Shell? Have you got your flat sorted yet? We'll have to do a proper tea and catch up when you've got time. I'm free Tuesday and Friday, though obviously if we do Tuesday I can't drink because of work, gross.*

Let me know! Love ya xoxo

When I get a message like that, I forget about the days I spent with a knot in my stomach, chewing on fingernails. And then, of course, an hour before meeting:

Btw gotta leave early because I said I'd do cocktails with the work lot but we'll still grab some food and that. Love you! See you soon!!!

Obviously, I wanna kick off, say I'm not some bullshit back-up plan she can rush through, but expressing my disappointment always hurts me far more than it hurts Toni. I stomach the breadcrumbs and get ready regardless, thinking about how I could have taken that extra shift instead.

Toni likes to say I work for Shell, but I don't. I work the register at a petrol station up the highstreet. My boss likes me because I'm one of the few people who doesn't mind working holidays. Might as well. Twice the pay, and I can play my own music when the place is dead. Anyway, who am I having Christmas with? Who am I gonna snog on New Years? For me, the job couldn't be better, but Toni amps it up to all her friends out of second-hand embarrassment, trying to make it sound more impressive because she has a proper job doing… something with marketing? I tend to switch off when she talks about it. It's where she met Craig, her soon-to-be fiancé, who I obviously and unoriginally hate.

I know it's a cliché for me to hate Craig, and I wish he had a bit more about him so our relationship wouldn't be so generic, but he uses words like "synergy" unironically. He styles his hair like a bully from a 2000s American sitcom, lives in rolled up chinos, and calls me "mate" and "pal" when he talks to me like I'm one of the lads. Whenever I see him at one of Toni's nights out, he gets way too drunk, and she has to take him home. On her last birthday, he tried to start on someone. Apparently, this guy had pushed him

as he walked past and spilt his pint or something.
I reckon Craig just spilt it himself but whatever.
When Toni had managed to calm him down, he
stuck with me in the smoking area, nicking all my
rollies while he went on and on, chatting absolute
bullshit: "Sorry I got like that, pal, sorry, yeah,
but it's about RESPECT, you know. It's about
RESPECT." After that night, he felt we'd built a
rapport. I felt I could shank him and have absolutely no guilt about it.

He messaged me to ask for Toni's hand in
boring, heteronormative marriage:

*I know she doesn't really have a family or a dad to
ask permission, but I want to do things properly, and
she always said you was like her family. Do I have
your blessing?*

My blessing? And comparing me to her
father? I wanted to say to him, "Mate, I'm not her
surrogate dad, alright? Your girlfriend used to
lick my cunt." Course I told Toni so that the surprise would be ruined. Jokes on me, though. She
thought that was the sweetest thing in the world.

Toni stopped tapping and put her phone
down next to her, not away, just next to her, face
up so she could see the notifications coming in.

"Sorry, that was Sian. Wants to know what
I'm wearing for cocktails. Anyway though, down
to business! I am *so* fucking hyped! Are you
hyped for me?"

"What about?"

"Don't be stupid. About Craig! Bless him. I can't believe he asked your blessing. Going to so much effort…"

"A message."

"Well, you can't tell him that I know, although obviously thank you for telling me because otherwise he would have messed the whole thing up. Please, please, *please* make sure that when he proposes it's somewhere good. Maybe on a beach or like, a restaurant, but a nice restaurant, not a dingy Spoons or anything."

"Toni, babes, we're in a dingy Spoons right now."

"Yeah, but we used to be chavs, so it's fine. Anyway, we're here for a couple of plates and a catch up, but it's not exactly a proposal place, is it? And if he checks in with you about the ring, make sure it's actually, properly nice. I'm not gonna fuck with any nasty, Haribo-looking thing. I want something at *least* a grand, or I'm sending it back."

I sat across from her taking tiny sips of beer. Her new, plumped out lips changed the shape of her face. Her smile was genuine though. This was real excitement. I couldn't believe she was so excited about something so shallow and dull.

"What the fuck do I know about engagement rings? The last time I deliberately slipped something on my fingers, it was a knuckle duster."

"Aw, babe, not having much luck in the world of lesbo dating?" She'd gone back to tapping on her phone while she spoke, so I stayed quiet. The world of lesbo dating didn't include her now, apparently. Abandoned for the straight world of mediocre men and quality fucking rings.

I remembered when we used to lie next to each other at night, in multiple duvets on a single bed. She'd sing songs while I pretended to be the guitar and drums until she stopped singing to laugh. She'd turn around to place her head on my chest when she slept, right between my breasts so that it didn't hurt, and I would stay like that for hours, grateful to know that she never slept as well without me, and I never slept at all without her.

Her phone went down again.

"Say what you want about Craig, but he's got more money than sense."

"That's a good thing?"

"Well, it means he's definitely getting me a good ring, yeah. A diamond, maybe. A big one. But not so big it's tacky, you know what I mean?"

"Look, do we have to talk about Craig the entire time? This is meant to be a catch-up."

"But I thought we were… Fine. Whatever. I'm sorry. How are you?"

I shrugged. "I mean, alright."

"That's good talk, babes."

"Well, what exactly do you want me to say? It's not like my life's all that riveting."

"How's the flat?'

"I mean, yeah, it's fine. It's great."

After a year of sofa-hopping, the council had finally sorted me out somewhere to live. It was shit, like. The steps in the building were thick concrete, and I was on the fourth floor, so every time I ventured down, I felt a premature pang in my knees. It always smelt like weed, and there was mould on the ceiling, but fuck it. It was home. It'd been so long since I'd had a home that I loved my little shithole. When I got in after a drink, I'd feel so grateful to be home that after locking the doors I'd hug them, kiss my fingers, and then trace them across the walls. I wanted to say this to Toni. I was sure she'd understand. But then again, she'd got her own mortgage at twenty-six, a little new-build with slogans on the wall in swirly, beige fonts: "Home is where the wine is!" and "Chase your thoughts and change your world!"

Not quite "Live, Laugh, Love" but close enough.

"You're not exactly giving me much, here. Come on! You know I love that interior design shit."

"Okay, well first off, there's no interior design. I don't have enough money to waste on photo frames and all that crap. But it's actually pretty great," I said, feeling myself start to smile. "I mean, it's a miserable place like, especially compared to your spare room…"

"It misses you greatly, just so you know."

"I miss it too. Not as much as your bedroom, obviously, but still. Nah, this new place feels special though, you know? It's, like, a total fucking shithole, but it's mine. I can go out with just my coat if I want to. I mean look at me, right now. Look. I have my coat, and my wallet in my jeans, and my fags and my phone, that's it. That's all I need. The other stuff, it's all tucked up at home safe. I finished a book the other day on shift, and I was like, right I'll leave it at Beth's, and she can read it and then I was like, you know what? Nah. I'll take it home. I can keep it now. It's not a burden to have things anymore, you know? It's not baggage to carry around."

Just as I'd started smiling, Toni had stopped.

"Listen, can you not say stuff like that?"

"Stuff like what?"

"Stuff like that. About my bedroom. The last time was ages ago…"

"It was a year ago."

"Two years, actually, but yeah."

"So what? We're just gonna pretend I never slept in your bed?"

"Yeah, 'cause I'm not like that. I wasn't even like that then. I was just a kid without a family, and the hostel was less scary with you on my side…"

"So I was a prison butch?"

"No. Obviously not. I just wish you wouldn't talk about stuff like that so casually, like it was normal. It's not like you're my ex or anything. You're the girl I hooked up with when I was homeless, when I didn't have a family to come and rescue me."

"That's not even true," I scoffed. "I mean if that was it, I'd get it. No one likes to be reminded of their trauma. You don't have to tell *me*…"

Although, actually, me and Toni were different like that. I wore my trauma on my sleeve. I shaved my head and tattooed my arms because I liked to make people uncomfortable, especially posh pricks with no clue. When people asked about my family, I'd say I don't speak to them. When they asked me why, I'd look them straight in the eyes: "Daddy touched me up, and Mummy did fuck all about it." There'd always be silence then. Well, fuck 'em. They should've minded their own business. It wasn't news to me, so why should I pretend to find it awkward? Nothing awkward about it, just the truth. Toni wasn't like that, though. She didn't want anyone to know.

Back in the hostel, everyone bragged about how bad they had it, the worse the better, and Toni was no exception. The place was filled with girls talking about daddies who beat them and:

At least your daddy's alive. Mine got killed when I was four.

Yeah, well, mine could be anyone. My mum works round back of Staples, and she's been trying to get me in the business from the beginning.

Yeah, well, mate, at least you know your mum…

It was an environment that these days would be called "toxic." Actually, it wasn't even safe. Outside the place was crawling with perverts ready to offer booze and cigs in exchange for blowjobs, which they obviously got. The girls *sort of* looked out for each other, in their own way. Me and Toni were roommates, so no one fucked with us, even if Toni liked to make out I was the butch, the bitch who had nails that could fuck up the best of them. And no one else could compete with her story.

"Yeah? You think that's bad? Aw, babies…" she'd begin, and everyone would look at her with wide eyes and morbid curiosity, ready to hear the worst of it.

Toni was left in a skip when she was born. She was found crying her heart out, having caught pneumonia, and the doctors didn't think she'd make it. That was a problem. Usually with babies, people jump to adopt, but not with Toni. Who would go through all the rigmarole of adopting a baby just to have it go and die on you? So, years hooked up to tubes in various hospitals, no one came looking for her, then years in foster homes. The hospital was the only place they didn't fuck with her. She even missed the little trays of food, which I think is part of the reason why she loves the tasteless Spoons grub. Finally, she got adopted by a mum and dad. Course, the step-brother tried to fuck with her in the shed behind the house, taught by his father, apple don't fall far, and the mum was one of them that just *loved* the attention she got from adopting a sick child. By the time Toni was 13, she was diagnosed with all sorts. Heart issues, lung issues, and a non-existent eating disorder. Course, if your mum doesn't let you eat because she wants to make it look like you've got a non-existent eating disorder, and if your pubescent body is causing you to get more attention than you ever wanted, you're gonna get properly sick after a while. Toni's body was full of self-harm scars. She'd burned herself with straighteners and, in a moment of true psychosis, attempted to cut off the flesh from her stomach. That psychotic episode was her saving grace. Back in her safe place, the hospital, she talked about good, old big bro, and back in the foster homes she went. It wasn't ideal. No one wanted a difficult, sick, teenage girl in their house, especially one that was so angry all the time. So, at fifteen, it was the hostels.

I was the only one who ever properly looked after her. I heard her story so many times, my arm around her shoulder, squeezing her for comfort whenever she got to a hard part, not that she ever showed an emotional reaction. Her eyes were always glazed as she spoke.

I can't remember exactly when she stopped bragging about her trauma. I'd like to say it was a side-effect of her new job, but it wasn't really. Her new job was more a side-effect of her brand-new, squeaky-clean attitude. There was the access course first, then the OU degree in business, then the job that I'm pretty sure was a pyramid scheme, then the inspirational posts shared on Facebook with little images of sunsets and trees. Suddenly, she didn't want to talk about her past anymore.

"I'm sick of embracing the victim narrative," she said. "My past doesn't define me."

"Narrative?" I'd asked. "What's narrative about it? You are a victim, aren't you? I mean, it fucking happened."

She shook her head at me as though I couldn't possibly understand, which pissed me off no end because I was the only one in her neat little circle of friends that could ever *begin* to understand.

And here she was again with that memory-wipe bullshit, the old "I'm not like that," that same insistence that if she just stopped talking about it, it'll all go away. She looked at me now, and I could see from the firm grip in her jaw that she felt she was setting a "necessary boundary." She went to counselling after her last break-up and learnt all these new terms that justified her selfishness. "Setting a boundary" was one. "Filling her own cup" was another. I took a big gulp of beer.

"Our relationship wasn't a bad thing," I said, just to end the silence.

"No. It wasn't, you're right, but you're focussing on the wrong word. You're focussing on *bad* when you should be focussing on *was*. It *wasn't* a bad thing, past tense. It *is* something different now. Now, you're my best friend. And we were meant to be having a catch-up, and you were meant to be helping me plan my engagement, but instead, all I'm getting is you dredging up the past."

Toni's eyes were wet, and I hated myself. I hated myself whenever I made her cry because all I wanted to do was throw my arms around her and hug her. I wanted to say "I'm sorry you're upset, and I'll get rid of that feeling right now, if I can. I'll take you away somewhere special. I'll never let anyone hurt you again. We can leave all the cunts behind and be safe." Though obviously I couldn't say that because this time I was the cunt that needed to be left behind.

"You know what I was going to ask you today?" Toni said, her throat choked. "Whether you wanted to be my maid of honour…"

"I don't want that."

"…because you're the most important person in my life, but fuck it. You're clearly still stuck in this victim mentality."

"Toni, it's not a mentality, okay? It's a massive part of who we are."

"Who we *were*, Tams." She stopped, swallowed, looked down at the table. She took a gulp of her cheap beer, almost like she would have done back when she was younger, parched for anything alcoholic and unconcerned about the quality.

The last time she'd looked like that was when Adam had dumped her. He was sick of her being clingy. On nights out, she was glued to his arm. If he spoke to anyone else, Toni would spend the entire time glaring at them across the room. Female friends were a no-no.

"Why does he have to talk to other girls? If he wants a feminine opinion, he can ask me," she explained once.

"Don't you think that's hypocritical?" I asked. "You still talk to me, don't you?"

"Yeah, but that's different. We're best mates. Basically family."

It took a while for Tones to accept that he'd left her. For ages, she just kept going to the same haunts, hanging out with his friends while she waited for him to show up.

"God, that Adam. He never looks at his phone," she'd say by way of explanation, and his mates would all stare into their drinks uncomfortably. Toni hadn't been invited, that much was obvious, but everyone was too awkward to remind her that she was just their pal's old missus, and they didn't understand why she kept turning up. I was dragged along as backup. I expect she probably knew that she looked a little deranged, and she needed at least one friend on her side to make it less uncomfortable.

It wasn't long before Adam moved on romantically, but then again, it wasn't exactly the whiplash betrayal that Toni made it out to be. Maybe a month? Two? He came along with Michelle, introducing her to everyone, no bother. He faltered over Toni and me but introduced us anyway, acting like it was absolutely fine that his ex still insisted on hanging around like a bad smell even though he'd blocked her number, even though half the time he hadn't bothered showing up for drinks himself. Michelle had obviously been told about Toni in advance, so she smiled sympathetically, and complimented her jacket, the only thing she could see above the table. *How sweet,* I thought. *She wants to make a good impression.* Toni, however, had not been pre-warned about Michelle.

"Adam," she said, "who the fuck is that?"

He sighed. "This is Michelle. From my gym."

"And what the fuck is she doing here?"

He looked at Michelle and half-shrugged, apologetically. Poor thing was frozen, her eyes all big in her face.

"Listen, Tones, shall we talk outside, yeah?" he attempted.

"What the FUCK is she doing here?"

I ended up taking Toni outside myself, wrangling in my arms. She'd been about to go for Michelle and, gym or not, that bird had no chance. Her arms were like bloody twigs. Toni's reputation was sealed then. The psycho ex. That had been the theory under the surface for a while now, but everyone was too British to mention it. I'd tried to tell her that we should stop going, that she needed to move on, but she'd just brush me off.

"You don't know boys. Their thing is that they don't actually know what they want."

It was a shame. I didn't actually mind Adam. I changed my mind that day though, when I saw him with his hands clasped behind his head, blowing out air while he muttered, "Mental! She's actually fucking mental!" as I got her out the door.

Well, yeah, I thought. *Course she is. Wouldn't you be?*

I took Toni to a bar one street over to calm down. She drank the wine like it was water, in big, deep gulps, and sobbed. It was obvious she hadn't believed that it was over, had thought if she manifested herself a nice, normal boyfriend and a nice, normal life then it was guaranteed to happen, but nah. Poor old Antonia Smith out of control yet again, the same baby girl left in a skip.

When the sobbing stopped and she was no longer too hysterical to speak clearly, the tears dripped down her cheeks as she stared at the floor.

"I loved him, you know," she said. "I really did."

I took Toni home that night and wrapped her up in bed. The next day we were back to how we'd been in the hostel, me between the sheets again, singing together in the shower, giggling like teenagers as we snuggled up in front of the telly. She went back to wearing my t-shirts. Officially, if anyone asked, I stayed in the spare room, but to be honest, I only stepped foot in there once or twice before she started seeing Craig.

Her eyes had that same look now in our Spoons that they'd had at the bar drinking wine after Michelle. She wasn't angry at all. She was sad, and there was nothing she could do about that sadness. I could have killed myself for being the one who put that look in her eyes.

"Look alright, I'm sorry," I began.

"You know I love you, don't you?"

"Yeah, I know that," I said. "I love you too. More than anything."

"But I need to close this chapter of my life. I can't keep going back to this."

"What are you talking about? 'Close this chapter.' Is that some more counselling bullshit?" Her phone buzzed next to her, and she picked it up. I rolled my eyes. "I've got to go now. I'm meeting the girls."

"You've not even had anything to eat yet. Come on."

Toni smiled at me. The cheeks were wet again. She leant over the table to kiss me. It wasn't open-mouthed with tongues flicking everywhere like it was when we were teenagers, but it wasn't the fake, platonic smack on the cheek she gave me whenever we were around other people either. It was soft and only slightly parted, and I knew that she was saying goodbye.

I guess that's when I started crying too. Our foreheads touched, and I wanted to say every-thing I'd ever felt about her, but I couldn't think of how to word it right, so instead I said something stupid and insincere:

"You know you're coming back, right? As soon as it doesn't work out with Craig, or you stop liking this job, or the meds stop doing the trick, you'll be back hitting me up and wanting to nick my old t-shirts again?"

Toni laughed a little through the tears. "I guess so, yeah. But let's hope it doesn't come to that."

"I love you more than anything."

"I know," she said. "I know."

Before she left, Toni went to the loo to reapply her make-up. She pretended not to see me as she walked out the exit and down the street. You wouldn't be able to tell that she'd been crying. Her face was a Maybelline mask. She shook her blonde waves so they dangled down her back and clicked away in her stilettos. I wondered, not for the first time, how she could strut so confidently on such uneven terrain.

Fuck 'em up, Lavinia

In another world, in another time, Lavinia would bite the lips off anyone who tried to hurt her. She'd smash their heads against the door until their skulls resembled pomegranate. She'd pick up her machete and get ready for revenge, and we would cheer for her with popcorn in our (still existent) hands.

In another world, in another time, Lavinia would fill bathtubs with lye; she'd dunk in their faces and put blades between their thighs. Lavinia would take fish hooks, let the birds pluck out their eyes, and we would hide behind our (again, yes, still existent) hands.

In another world, in another time, Lavinia would grow into her modified prosthetics. She'd hold a cigarette between the metal claws and rest her forearm on the knees of survivors while they cried, and we would know that she had seen far worse and lived (if at least hypothetically) to tell the tale. In another world, in another time, Lavinia would decide her own worth beyond her father's diagnosis of damaged goods. Lavinia would know she was more than a mangled cat better to be put out of its misery. She would navigate her new reality, an exemplar of recovery.

In another world, in another time, Lavinia would refuse to squash herself into the mould of victimhood carved out for her. She would never let those bastards see her wander through the world, mute and left in agony. She'd use her bloody stumps to spell out accountability. She'd take their flesh and grind it into mincemeat and feed it to the mothers who defend their little monsters, and she would feel nothing but the satisfaction of a long-forgotten vigilante.

And, God love her, she would make them fucking eat it.

Futility

Katie awoke to the sound of ocean waves. It wasn't the real ocean, but an alarm she'd downloaded to encourage relaxation and calm. She liked to pretend she was *at one* with nature. Nothing could be better, she opined, than rising with the sun and listening to waves gush against fictitious sand.

Katie didn't need to get up at 6:30 today, but she did anyway. The last time she'd mistakenly checked her phone, it had been 2 a.m., meaning that today she'd have to cope with around four hours of sleep unless she abandoned the idea of self-improvement altogether, but Katie needed to get into *routine*. In the dark and dirty days, she would sleep until noon on a Saturday, and even then she'd be hungover and tired despite the hours and hours of rest. It was better to be the sort of person who woke up with the sun and faced the day ready and raring to go. The transitional stages were difficult, but still, she was driven. She was prepared.

Katie extracted herself from the bedsheets at 6:45. She would start the day with thirty minutes of meditation and self-reflection. This would allow her to face people with kindness, mindfulness, and compassion, improving not only her own mental health but the mental health of those surrounding her, although they were admittedly few. Again, she listened to the sound of ocean waves, but this time they were accompanied by chimes and the calming tones of an American woman who told her to count her breath and envision a golden light gradually spreading up from her toes to the top of her head. Katie thought about her exhaustion. Her mind wandered to the shopping she had to do, the plants she had to water, the bills piling up on her desk, but she stopped and scolded herself. She was supposed to be thinking of nothing until she reached a new spiritual mentality. *Nirvana.* She placed her hands in a prayer position and raised them to her forehead, gently pressing the sides of her thumbs into her third eye. She whispered the few Hindi words she knew: *Namaste, Svagata, Shavasana, Pyjama...*

7:15. Katie made her bed, opened the curtains, and watered her plants. She padded barefoot to the kitchen and checked the magnetic whiteboard attached to her fridge. Today, breakfast was a banana and kale smoothie. This particular treat had the liquefied disappointment of not being a real meal while also maintaining a stodgy consistency which made her feel sick half-way through the chugging. She whizzed the ingredients together in her blender and downed it with her nose pinched. She tried to find her inner smile. Katie had read that those who lived consistently on a healthy diet eventually found fried food oily and repellent. She thought of crispy hash-browns and asked herself if she felt repelled. Tragically, she didn't.

Breakfast takeaways had been a regular habit of the dark and dirty Katie. She'd wake up delighted it was already past 11 so she could order a delivery of bacon sandwiches, fry-ups in polystyrene boxes, chow-meins with egg fried rice... On a good day, there'd still be half a box of cheesy chips or cold pizza left for her to gobble up. She'd half-jokingly call it recycling.

8:00. She wondered if she should go for a run, although it wasn't necessary because she had her cross-fit class later, so instead, she showered. Katie was proud of how she showered. Shampoo bars, apricot scrubs from metal tins, and energising shower gels from recycled squeezy bottles. She washed her skin like she was trying to scrape it off, imagining her tiredness could be abated with cleanliness and good intentions. Katie always stayed too long in the shower. Sometimes she'd listen to music and sing, forcing the dopamine to release itself on the shake of her vibrato, but today, she showered in silence. Her eyes felt heavy and her nose was stuffed up. She stepped on the scales to see if she'd lost weight. Not yet.

She wanted to be just under 9 stone, but she was 9 stone 7 and appalled by the way fat was hanging off her hips. When she grabbed the skin on her arm, there was a substantial amount of flesh between her fingers like a slab of rubber. She'd been 11 stone in the dark and dirty days. This was better, but she still had far to go.

Towel dried, soft trousers, baggy t-shirt, matching socks, and comfy trainers, Katie tried not to wear make-up if she could help it. Miraculously, it was already 9:00. Time passed so quickly while Katie showered and got ready for the day. Sometimes removing the towel proved too difficult, and she would sit on the end of her bed feeling contemplative and numb for hours. Other times, she wandered from place to place looking for her socks, her pants, her contact-lens solution but never settling efficiently. The only thing that got her up and stopped her staring into space was the thought of food.

Meals were always meticulously planned. The whiteboard told her there was leftover chili for lunch and salmon and spinach for tea (Katie avoided carbs where she could help it). That meant she just had to visit the fishmonger and the farmer's market

The sun was up when Katie left her apartment block, but it was still early enough for the air to be cool and refreshing. Since she'd binned the fags, Katie could more easily smell the grass, the trees, the car pollution. Her tiredness made the day seem distant and ethereal. Sobriety was often as disorientating as drunkenness.

Her canvas bag was decorated with a sunflower. On bad days, she bought herself flowers as a reminder that she didn't need the approval of others and could love herself twice as effectively. She wondered if today was a bad day. Nothing terrible had happened to her, but she still felt the need for flowers. There was a lump in her throat as she walked down the sunshiny street. She counted out her errands: salmon, spinach, fruit, flowers…

Katie had stopped seeing her friends months ago. She could never meet them for a few drinks without taking it too far, without smoking too many cigarettes and eyeing up old men. She couldn't talk to them without saying something embarrassing. They still texted her sometimes. They asked if she wanted to do coffee or maybe shopping, something that wouldn't impact on her new, healthy regime, but Katie was cutting out caffeine, and she didn't want to waste money on things she didn't need, so she ignored the texts. They were never good friends. They undermined her achievements. They bought tequila shots.

Toxic. That's what they were. Katie read that phrase in a self-help book called *Becoming Free*. She pretended she loved that book, told people in the office that it was her new Bible, but the reality was she hadn't much enjoyed reading it. There was some vindictive satisfaction in recognising toxicity, being able to point at people and know they were representative of all that was incorrect. At the end though, there was little resolution. While she knew what was wrong with everyone else, there was no solution regarding how to fix it. She placed the book on the coffee table in front of her, finished her green tea, and tried to reflect on it all. Strange how when attempting to meditate, she couldn't turn her mind off, but when trying to reflect, all was silent.

19:45. Katie was running to crossfit, late again because, like a child, she didn't finish her spinach. She'd stared at the mush on her plate feeling ill, thinking that if she didn't eat it now, she wouldn't have the energy for later, and she already felt so tired as it was. Eventually, she had to leave it. She hoped that her exhaustion after the class would be enough to make her fall asleep as soon as her head hit the pillow. Sometimes that happened and offered her some sort of respite. Often it didn't.

She called her pre-crossfit run a "warm-up." It helped her feel empowered, she said, although it also made her sweaty and red-faced. She wondered if other people in the class found her inspiring or irritating. She didn't care. It was good to be keen, and she was keener than anyone, often pulling muscles. The trainer had taken her aside last week: "It's not always a competition, Katie," he'd said, and when she'd jokingly replied "Yes, it is!" too loudly, hoping that he'd laugh, he had merely looked concerned.

Her gym was on the sea-front and relatively expensive. An outdoor pool was visible from the outside and a running track lay just below her. Now, she was on the pier and could see her gym in the distance looking deceptively close. She needed to rest. She would faint if she didn't. Katie stopped by the railings on the pier and stared down at the ocean. There was usually a rocky beach beneath, but at this time of night, the tide was in, and all she could see were the waves hitting the concrete pier below her. The white foam reminded her of lager. She wanted a drink more than anything else in the world.

Katie didn't want to give up. She really didn't. It had been months, and she'd worked so hard, and there was still so much to accomplish. There were eight pounds left to lose, milestones to hit at work, and therapeutic books on her nightstand that she hadn't finished reading. She remembered the dark and dirty Katie who embarrassed herself at work-dos, who no one really liked because she was fat and spotty and loud. That Katie deserved what happened to her, but this new Katie didn't. This Katie was trying so hard to be better. Katie needed to go to the gym. She needed to get to her class. Her legs were jelly, and she tasted something like blood in the back of her throat. Her lungs were heavy. She needed sleep, but she couldn't skip the class because then none of these months of hard work would be worth it. She needed to do this, to stick to the new routine in the hope that one day everything would click together, and she'd have the right brain, the right body, the right mind-set, and finally she'd get to feel the happiness that everybody else did.

But Katie knew it wasn't the drinking and it wasn't the smoking or the drugs or the promiscuity which had made her so miserable and destructive. It wasn't the dodgy diet or the few extra pounds. There was something intrinsic within her that was wrong, and it couldn't be burned off, or meditated away, or washed clean with apricot body scrub in a too long, too hot shower. She watched the waves crashing into the bottom of the pier as the lingering tourists hung around taking in the views. Katie stared into the depth and wondered if there was anything, any course of action that would make it all worth it.

She ended her life with a leap and a crunch into the sound of the ocean waves.

Jerks

The gang group-wank in a circle for the joy of seeing one unlucky fucker have to eat the spunk. Each boy cums onto a cracker, spreads their substance like butter, and then they tower them together to make one substantial snack. Cum has a glueing agency. This, they all know well.

Unlucky Fucker doesn't mind. In fact, he deliberately strokes himself with a loose grip so he can sample it, the salty, milky taste of all his friends, with their muscled shoulders and flat stomachs and gentle, skinny cocks. They play football together. They look good. The parents of these boys are (mostly) very proud. All of them, they are certain, will get into a good college. God willing, they may end up in the same fraternity.

The boys are all separate people with different hopes, thoughts, and ambitions, but they try not to let that get to them too much. The boys communicate through mocking laughter, grunts, and curses. These techniques set a tone of affection without distracting them from their video games.

One of the boys likes alternative 90s music, so they decide it would be easier if they all like alternative 90s music. They nod along to Offspring, Blink 182, and Soundgarden's "Black Hole Sun." The ones who *choose* to like alternative 90s music, but who are unlikely to have come to it naturally, have realised it's hard to dislike a song when you know all the words. The one who *really* likes alternative music keeps the Elliott Smith to himself.

In their own unique ways, every boy finds comfort in the dank, grey cellar where they hang out for their circle jerks. There's one long leather sofa and a good setup for gaming. When they sit together, their thighs rub against each other, especially when they're concentrating and leaning forward, their knees are bouncing erratically up and down, until they get a text saying it's getting late, and it's a school night, and one by one they drop off back to their own single beds, uncased pillows, and Bob Marley posters hanging like Christ above them. It is notable that none of these boys have ever listened to reggae.

One boy, who's less sporty than the others, although he still plays football and doesn't hate it as much as he used to, is probably going to pick a science major. The gang end up on the football field after school, sit around with weak cans of beer and blankets over their knees while they watch Science Boy set up three-litre soda bottles with Mentos. It stops being funny when they're cold and they're sticky, and then the sun goes down and they kind of want to go, but he's got firelighters. These are better than the soda bottles, which were pathetic in the end, doing little but leaving soggy patches all over the grass. The firecrackers at least have the decency to explode, which makes up for the prior disappointment and means the rest of the boys don't err towards regret.

None of the gang like *Jackass*, but somewhere down the line, it was assumed by each that the rest of the gang liked *Jackass* so now they all pretend to like *Jackass* to fit in. After watching fish-hooks placed through face-cheeks and dicks branded onto ass-cheeks, they each go home (except, of course, Cellar Boy, whose house it is, and who intends to smoke a joint on his leather sofa first), and crawl into their musty bedsheets and think about how much that shit would hurt. They tuck their shafts between their legs for extra protection, devastated by the reality that the only

time their dicks get touched by anyone but themselves is when their pals backhand them as a joke.

At one point, the Unlucky Fucker who always
ends up eating cum stands up from the leather
couch. It's the summer holidays, and the boys
didn't end up in the same fraternity or even the
same colleges. It's August now, and it's so hot
his thigh-skin peels when he stands. The others
turn to look at him, wondering if he's going to
the bathroom or to the kitchen to get another beer,
but his eyes are clenched shut, and he eventually says:

"You three are the only people I've ever
truly loved."

Mostly they're bemused and uncomfortable,
although there's an inkling of gratitude from
Alternative Music boy who was always the most
sensitive of the bunch. Science Boy breaks the
silence when he says:

"Don't be fucking gay, dude."

And Unlucky Fucker shrugs and sits
back down.

The others turn back to the screen where
they're killing zombies and wish that he *had*
been getting a beer because now they're all
feeling thirsty.

For the first time in a long time, that night the Unlucky Fucker doesn't eat the cum. He wants to, but he reckons it'll be the last time he'll do this for a while and the excitement gets to him too quickly. In the end, he's the third to cum. It's gobbled up by Cellar Boy who doesn't enjoy it but understands that fair is fair and, as host especially, considers it only proper to acquiesce.

September comes. The boys miss each other. No one says a thing about it, but for the first week of college, they all add extra salt to their food.

Le Laurier Rose

Something was amiss. The rings were gold in *colour*, but that was where all resemblance ended. The so-called diamonds hung heavy and dull against her neck. A shadow of green tainted her earlobes. I glanced from her shoes (heeled with a diamante strap) to her head (brown, frizzy hair greying at the roots, lips pursed and painted red with something I doubted was a cosmetic in the traditional sense). The lines around her mouth told tales of a lifetime of smoking.

"May I help you, Madame?"

"The service here is despicable. Hours I've been waiting for a table. Famished. *Not* the kind of treatment I would expect from such an establishment."

I smiled slightly in apology, but I had my second sign then that something was amiss. Her accent was affected and comically old-fashioned. The extra "h" sound after the "w" in "waiting" showed me that she understood what sounds were meant to be refined but had no idea exactly where to place them.

"Of course, my apologies. Do you have a reservation with us?"

"I hardly think that will be necessary. I'll take my regular table."

I nodded politely, suddenly conscious that this woman wasn't just delusional in the new-money sense but clinically insane. I had worked upwards of two decades at Le Laurier Rose, evidenced by my receding hairline and the wrinkles around my eyes. Not that I minded ageing. I felt I managed it with grace, maintaining my slim figure and seeming tall and distinguished rather than plump and tired, as so many men in their forties do. Of course, I had never seen this woman before in my life.

"Right this way, Madame."

I placed her at one of our more comfortable tables, near the window facing our garden. A water feature danced beautifully when it was lit up at night, although at this hour of the morning, it was far less impressive. Thankfully, the bright, green turf made up for whatever mysticism the daylight lacked.

"A drink?" I asked.

"Yes." She paused. "What would you recommend?"

I smiled, knowing I'd have liked to recommend a visit to the neurologist or at the very least a hairdresser.

"Depending on the appetiser, I might suggest a Cabernet Sauvignon, or perhaps a Sauvignon Blanc?"

"Champagne?" she asked hopefully. I chuckled.

"But of course, champagne will go well with anything. Our house is a wonderful Dom Pérignon." My attempt at sarcasm failed.

"Right, well, yes. I suppose that will do." She unfolded the swan napkin and laid it across her lap, smoothing it down anxiously.

"One moment, Madame."

Thankfully, it was around 10 a.m. and too early for a lunch crowd, so I had time to find, pop, and pour the glass with an effortless smile before fitting in a tactful summoning of the police. After a brief description in which I tried to be as forgiving as possible (a considerable effort), I managed to detach myself from the excited operator, who was still babbling on when I hung up the phone:

"Okay, from what you're saying this fits the description of a missing person. The police are on their way, but sir…"

"Merci beaucoup," I interrupted, as the missing person we were discussing was now standing in front of me. I hung up the phone as gracefully as possible. "Yes, Madame, is there something else I might help you with?"

"Toilet?" she asked, and again I smiled. Of course, she would say "toilet" and not "loo" or "lavatory." With her accent so needlessly posh, she may as well have asked for the "shitter," and it would have had the same effect.

"Just this way, Madame."

She was in there too long. I stood polishing the glasses, staring at the cursive font across from me, worrying that she might have escaped, and I'd needlessly bothered the police for the price of a glass of champagne. Although, I must admit, the thought of her escaping did bring some small relief. While I found the woman amusing for now while it was quiet, who knew what trouble she might stir up when the real customers arrived? But she returned after around fifteen minutes, emerging from the ladies' room, smelling thickly of our personal spray, her Crayola lipstick reapplied. Her hair had been moistened and flattened down which, good lord, only served to emphasise the frizz, making her appear like a balding man or, even worse, a circus clown. She settled down at her table again, and I came to take her order. There were no other customers, so it would have been strange if I didn't.

"Anything to start, Madame?"

"Yes," she sighed. "I had scampi once. It might have been here. I can't remember. It was delicious."

"In that case, might I suggest the fishcakes to start? Made with freshly caught cod and locally sourced salmon, lightly battered in breadcrumbs, served with our hollandaise sauce?"

"Yes." She nodded, smiling. "Yes. That would be lovely. Will it go with the, um, the champagne?"

I laughed gently. "Madame, I've yet to meet a dish that doesn't go well with champagne."

She laughed herself then, cautiously at first and then in longer, louder bellows. "Yes, quite right, good chap. Quite right."

After taking her main order too, I was left with a quandary. Did I or did I not place the order with the kitchen? If she was taken away, it would be such a waste of time and money. In my head, however, I already had an understanding of how the situation would play out. I imagined the upset daughter who would come to retrieve this woman, probably looking both guilty and harassed. No doubt that she would offer to pay, this imaginary woman in her forties, clicking along in her heels and writing a cheque while she apologised for her poor senile mother who was often going out and doing things like this. But then, the mad woman may well be under the care of the state, in which case we were doomed. I doubted the government stretched to buy Michelin star meals for mental-cases. I decided to order anyway. Without knowing how long they'd be to collect her, it would be suspicious if she was waiting for hours with no food, especially since there were no other customers to speak of.

"Fish cakes and sirloin…" I shuddered before continuing, "well done."

"Bit early, innit?" our chef, Michael, asked. He had tattoos creeping up his arms, neck, and face, and for some reason, it was felt this enhanced his credentials. His sous chef wiped down the already spotless steel.

"A surprise customer came without a reservation."

"Celebrity?"

I scoffed. "Hardly. I've called the police to collect her, but an order's an order."

"If you say so. Worst comes to worst, it'll be my mid-morning snack."

I nodded curtly and went back to pour the mad woman another glass of champagne.

She had time for the starter, which she finished with relish, her spoon scraping the bottom of the plate, but hardly had the sirloin touched the pan when the police arrived. And what a ruckus! There were three cars in total. The lights and sirens were alight and blaring. The officers all had batons tucked into their belts. I wondered if my customer had noticed, but she sat, untroubled, staring out into the garden. She continued to smile. She smoothed down her napkin. There was no time to greet the (eight!) police officers who rushed over to her.

"Alright, Christine. It's time to come with us," one said firmly, already in the process of restraining her.

"Who are you?" she asked indignantly. "If you don't mind, I am trying to enjoy my lunch."

"We can do this the easy way or the hard way. Come on."

It looked very much to me as though they were already attempting to do things the hard way, but she sighed and stopped resisting.

"Oh very well." She stood and was immediately cuffed. Her body was thrown, not particularly nicely, against the table. "I mean, really," she scoffed, and I couldn't help but think the same.

"Can someone please explain what's happening?" I asked the nearest officer. She was a young girl, red hair tired up into an elaborate plaited bun. She wasn't wearing any makeup, and I couldn't help but think she seemed too pale.

"Are you the one who rang us?" she asked.

"Yes, but all the same…"

"This is Christine Powell. The murderer."

I froze. A cliché I know, and I wish that it hadn't, but unfortunately, my blood did run cold. A thousand questions ran through my head, too panicked to be clearly articulated. How close had I been to death? How close to endangering our staff? How could I have handled this so recklessly?

"My God," I said. "Who did she kill?"

But at this point, the pale police officer was walking away with the others as they wrangled Christine through the back entrance and into the police car.

"We'll obviously be closing this area for a while," another officer said to me.

"But we have lunch reservations."

"Well, I doubt it'll last that long. We just have to get her back to prison, and then we can reopen the roads."

"Prison." I laughed. "She's in prison."

"She *was*," he said. "Broke out about a week ago. God knows how. We found her tracksuit in a skip outside the suburbs."

I cringed, thinking of how brutally I'd belittled her outfit. I suppose she'd done her best with a bad job. "Right," I said. "One moment."

I rushed back to Michael in the kitchen. Of course, he and his sous chef hadn't heard a thing. Chefs are amazing for their ability to recognise the slightest hint of incorrect spicing while simultaneously being completely unaware of the world outside their hectic little steam sphere.

"No need for the sirloin," I said.

"Fuck's sake, it's done. And far too overcooked for any of us lot to enjoy." Michael threw down his spatula. It was a generally accepted fact, also, that the angrier the chef, the better the food. "Done a runner?"

"Sort of," I began. "She's being arrested. She's a murderer."

"Oh, fuck!" Michael shouted.

His sous chef stopped dicing potatoes. "You're kidding?"

"I wish I was." I laughed and realised then how jittery I felt. My reflection in their metal stove-backs was pasty. I looked unwell.

"Well, who is she?"

"Pauline or Christine something. I don't know."

"Not Christine Powell?" the sous chef asked. He grabbed his phone from his apron pocket, unlocking it to scroll. "I've heard of her." He ran his hand over his beard, although it was covered in its neat little blue net.

"I think that was her name, yes. I don't know."

He whistled to himself.

"What is it?"

"I knew I'd heard of her. She's all over the news."

"What did she do?" Michael asked.

"Well, she escaped."

"Before that, you daft twat."

I smirked. This kind of aggressive masculinity was something that escaped my understanding. Not for the first time, I was grateful to be on the other side of the swinging doors.

"I dunno yet! There's all this debate at the moment about letting the dangerous ones out of maximum security even when they've been in decades. I'm just finding…" A pause.

"Well, fuck me," said sous chef (Tom? John? The turnover was so fast here).

"What?" I asked, hating this suspense, hating more that I would never *dream* of having a phone in my work apron, but at this moment, I so desperately wanted to be able to search for myself.

"She ate the bodies."

"Fuck off!" Michael shouted. I swallowed to stop myself vomiting. Tom/John read robotically from his phone, and while I heard the words, they didn't quite register until far later, a peculiar sensation like inverted déjà vu.

"'Christine Powell was working as a house and groundskeeper for the Maxwell family when she killed, cooked, and ate them on December 23rd, 1984. She had asked for a live-in position after the coal strikes impacted her living situation, and she was left without heating. When the Maxwells declined, she bludgeoned them to death with Clive Maxwell's Social Enterprise in Wealth and Society award. She killed his wife, Shirley Maxwell, and two children, Josephine and Oscar, in the same manner, before hacking off their limbs and roasting them to eat. She was arrested ten days later when Maxwell's business partners reported him missing. Powell was found wearing Shirley's clothes and jewellery, insisting that she was the rightful owner of the property. The family's remains were found in various soups and stews…'"

Tom/John stopped reading. I wished the kitchen didn't smell so much like soup. A killer. A cannibal. I'd given her champagne.

"Fucking hell. Glad she didn't have the steak in the end," Michael continued. "I'm good, like, but I don't think I can make cow taste better than human." Tom/John laughed, and I backed out of the door.

Not that outside the kitchen was much better. I didn't understand how it could take so long to organise an arrest. The officers were still milling around, even though Powell must have been clasped tightly in the backseat of their car already.

"Were you the one that rang us?" a different police officer said, this one short and slightly overweight, old enough to have been on the original case, I would imagine.

"Yes," I said stiffly.

"We'll need a statement."

"Of course, sir. Right this way."

I sat him down at the nearest table, this one facing out into the street. I kept looking at the line of police cars, wondering where she was and what she might have been thinking when she was uncuffed and sat here, right in my bludgeoning vicinity.

I told the story from beginning to end, leaving out some of the more needless details.

"Did you recognise her picture?" the officer asked me.

"No," I said. "No, I've only just now learned who she is. Did she really kill and *eat* that poor family."

The officer nodded. "Big time. She had Clive Maxwell's flanks for the Christmas roast, slathered in Bisto gravy apparently."

"Christ." I winced. Michael really needn't have worried about the quality of the steak; the woman clearly had no taste.

"If you didn't recognise her, how did you know to call us?"

I paused. What way was there to explain the plastic earrings? The awful diamante strap?

"I don't know. Gut feeling. She didn't seem like she belonged here. I thought she might do a runner."

"Good instinct." The officer nodded approvingly. "You've done half our work for us." He stood to leave. The rest of the officers had started to file out too and were waiting by the pavement.

"Listen," I began, thinking about how smug I'd been when I'd had no idea she was so dangerous. It must have shown on my face. She must have noticed. "I don't mind admitting I'm quite shaken up here. If she got out once, she can get out again. What if she comes for me? I mean I'm the one who rang you. She knows where I work. I..."

"I wouldn't worry if I were you." The officer shook his head. "Lightning doesn't strike twice. She's not gonna be getting out of max for the rest of her days. Anyway, even if she did get out, you'd be the *last* person she'd want to hurt."

"Why?" I asked.

"I dunno, mate. You must be good at your job; she asked us to pass on her thank yous."

"She said *thank you*?"

"Oh, she said more than that, she practically waxed lyrical about you. You must be the first person that's ever acted like she's the posh bint she pretends to be. Anyway, ta-ra. We'll keep you informed if there's any changes, but this should be quickly resolved now."

He walked away. With my statement taken, they could leave, I suppose. I followed him out, desperately needing fresh air. Michael and Tom/

John were also there by the kitchen exit, smoking cigarettes and watching the drama unfold. Michael held up his hand to me, and I waved back. I turned to look at the cars. In the last one, I could see her, just. It was hard through the tinted windows, but there was definitely the shape of her frizzy hair, flattened at the top. For some reason I don't know, perhaps to protect myself even further, I waved to her too. I thought I saw her wave back.

When they'd all driven off, there was an eerie quiet. Of course, the roads were closed. I leant back against the brick wall as I listened to sirens slowly disappearing.

It was nothing, really. It would be an eventful story to tell at dinner parties. People would gasp in shock and slight amusement. *You saw her? In the flesh!* Tabloids might contact me, but I would turn them down. Still, I felt slightly despondent. There was a profound sadness to it all. I suppose it was just the adrenaline rush fading.

I returned inside to wipe the tables. It was nearly noon, and the lunch rush would flood in soon. The customers would be famished, and I'd have a job to do.

Newborn

Meredith described the weather as "bipolar," apparently with no hint of irony. The sky was split into two distinct shades of blue, and we shivered, soaking wet beneath the sun. We reached the cemetery fence. Its black metal spikes looked good for impaling heads. Meredith forced a smile.

"Look, it's brightening up," she said. "Maybe we should call the baby Sky."

We were on a name-finding mission. Apparently, tombstones were good inspiration for when you were stuck. Meredith was wearing her baggiest dress, long and grey over her fishnets, but it was superfluous. Her bump was barely distinguishable. The only way you could tell she was pregnant was by the sudden clearing up of her teenage acne. Meredith was as fresh-faced and radiant as an angel beneath her dyed-black, rain-flattened hair. We wandered through the open gate onto a gravel path.

"Doubt you'll find any Skys in here." I scoffed, reading along the row of mossy graves. "These are all old-people names. Look: Alfred."

"Some of them are nice," Meredith said. "Johnathon… Benedict…." She trailed off when we reached a Gerald. "Anyway, it might be a girl."

All morning I'd been bored and wet. Normally on a weekend, we'd be with the lads drinking cider and smoking spliffs under the bridge by the beck, but now it was just us two, and Meredith didn't want to have fun anymore. In her newfound condition, she'd decided to embrace wholesome femininity. This was why she wasn't wearing her usual goth make-up, why she'd worn her floatiest dress, why she said we should meet up at 10 today instead of the usual 3 or 4. Occasionally, her hand would stroke her stomach like a sleeping cat. I put my hands in my pocket, checking that the stolen cigarette was still waiting for me in my leather jacket. I frowned. It was getting increasingly bent, but I had to wait until Meredith got bored of this maternity bullshit before I could have a smoke.

"You know whatever name you choose, it'll have to go with Beaver." I smirked.

Meredith winced. "No, I don't think so. The baby's mine. I'll give it my name."

Joshua Beaver was Meredith's long-term boyfriend. They'd been together two years, an absolute lifetime to me who couldn't seem to make a boyfriend last more than four months before getting bored and sacking them off for someone different. I definitely wouldn't have let Josh last very long. He was a nineteen-year-old wet wipe who stunk of weed and Monster. He thought he was a good metal vocalist because he could pig squeal, but he wasn't. I'd seen his band play at a pub once. We snuck in, got fake IDs, did our faces up. In the end, there were only about six people there, and his band was shit. I asked Meredith what she saw in such a BO-tainted gobshite, but she just shrugged.

"He's gentler than you think, especially when we're on our own."

I had my suspicions she only shagged him to cover her traces. That way if she smelt like cum, if she caught an itch between her thighs, if she got caught in Boots buying Vitamin D and gloopy mascara she didn't need to hide the pregnancy test in her basket; it was gossip but not a scandal. See, everyone called Meredith bipolar as a joke, but she was actually properly mental. Once she got caught trying to pierce her own nipple in the school toilet. Everyone found out when she got changed in PE, and the blood was seeping through her white, padded cup. Another time our old caretaker found her rolling around on the playing field naked and speaking in tongues. She got suspended for two weeks, and the school cut the grass shortly after. No more daisies and buttercups to roll about it, just the lovely, fresh scent of sliced nature. They claimed it was for rounders, but the timing was suspicious. Even at seventeen, she still regularly pretended she could speak to ghosts.

It made sense that Meredith was mental. Her dad had got barred at the Queen's Head for flashing a bunch of fifteen-year-old girls in the toilet. "Chris Royal's a nonce" is scratched on the doors of every cubicle, lest we forget. I asked Meredith about it one weekend when we were sitting by the beck. Emboldened by the cider and the tinny phone speaker music, I said: "Is it true your dad's a nonce?" And she scoffed and told me to fuck off, said the girls were lying about him because he'd asked them for ID when the bar-staff clearly didn't give a fuck.

But then that same night, she woke me up. It was another one of those nights where we were "sleeping over." We got away with murder with my mum as long as we woke up in the same house, so we'd stumble back from the beck at 3 a.m. and crash top and tail on my single bed while the TV buzzed blue playing old episodes of *Family Guy*. She shook me awake when I was happy and dozy and started telling me stories about her family. Not the sort of stuff you'd want to repeat. Never figured out if it was true or not. Hardly mattered. I just wanted to know how fucked up she really was, and in the blue glaze of the telly box, with her eyes dark rimmed and her voice all monotone, she let me know. You'd have to be pretty fucked up to say what she said, regardless of whether it was true. Afterwards, I spooned her back to sleep because she seemed a little needy, and when we woke up at midday, we said no more about it.

Now Meredith was nearly seventeen and pregnant which, if I'm honest, was the inevitable end for her. She seated herself cross-legged in front of a grave beneath the shade of a sapling. Her skirt spilled over her legs like a tablecloth.

"See this grave here?" she told me. "It's my mother's."

I looked at the smooth front of the tombstone. The grave was for an Ethel Truth who died in 1885.

"Sure it is," I said. "Is baby Ethel what you're thinking?"

"She died to have me, you know?" Meredith said. "She wanted to bring me into the world so much that she let herself bleed out trying. She sacrificed herself for me."

"That's tragic that," I said, but I'd already been told about her mum who died of lung cancer when Meredith was six. I'd seen her family photos. She looked just like Meredith but with blonde hair and skinny eyebrows. I knew her name was Claire.

"Maybe if she'd stayed alive, she could have taught me how to do it all. She would know how to help me with breast feeding and changing nappies. She'd tell me all the same tricks that worked for me would work for her granddaughter, and I would trust her. We would bond and understand each other in ways we hadn't before." Meredith picked up a twig from the ground and traced it along the dirt. It was the same pentagon she drew on everything absent mindedly, five slick lines you could do without looking. "But she's gone now. So who's going to help me raise this baby? Who's going to care?"

The sun went in behind some clouds. I looked up and realised how quickly they were moving across the sky, like they'd been sped up for the news. The wind was shaking the naked branches of the sapling. I squatted next to Meredith and put an arm around her shoulders.

"I'll help," I said. "I don't know much about kids, and I'm not touching any nappies, but I can help with all of the other stuff." She ignored my arm, the stick in the ground making squiggles that looked like some made up language, and the wind blew harder and whipped my hair into my lip-gloss. I extricated myself from Meredith to sort out the sticky strands. "Shall we go back to mine? Get a cup of tea? It's gonna rain again."

A twig snapped loudly above me. I looked up at the tree, but it was all in one piece. The grave of Ethel Truth, however, was cracked from top to bottom, and I didn't know if that was where the snapping sound had come from or whether it had been cracked before and I just hadn't noticed. I whispered "What?" before I looked down and saw that Meredith's drawing was cutting the ground *deep*. Those five lines were looking blacker and blacker against the brown dirt.

Meredith was speaking in tongues again. I always thought she did that for attention. It was the kind of thing that tended to happen whenever she wanted people to notice her, but this time I could hear the gibberish translated in my head, along with the roar of the wind. It was quiet and hard to hear, but somehow I understood completely.

Please protect this baby, please, please, do what's best for her, please don't let her suffer like I did, please don't let her suffer, please, please, please...

And as the wind rose, the whispers overlapped, and I could hear them all with Meredith's tongues, which turned into screams, into sobs.

The wind died down. The clouds stopped moving. The sun crept out again, and the trees stopped making a racket. Meredith was sobbing, and I pulled her into a hug.

"Hey," I said. "It's alright, it's alright."

I had no idea what had happened, but I knew something had shifted. Meredith had done something insane and magic, something I couldn't understand. She lifted up her baggy skirt for me.

"Has it happened?" she asked me. "I don't know if it's happened."

Underneath her fishnet tights, coating her pubic stubble and ingrown hairs and the lace of her Primark thong, blood was gathering on Meredith's thighs. It was thick and viscous, more brown than red.

"Yeah, don't worry," I told her. "It's happened."

"Oh baby," she cried again. "Baby girl, Ethel, oh baby."

The gravestone was still cracked from top to bottom. When I leant forward to inspect the mossy, old tombstone, I realised the date had changed. 2014.

On the way to Tescos, we shared twos on the fag in my pocket. Meredith looked like she could use it. We bought a pack of supermax pads and then toddled into the customer toilet so she could wash herself.

"The man at the corner shop fancies me," she said, rubbing her thighs with wet paper towels. "He'll probably serve us if you still wanna go to the beck." I did. The weather had cleared up completely now, and it would be a waste to just sit inside.

Now More than Ever

Hi there. It's me. Do you remember me? We met just fifteen minutes ago on this very same screen. How are you? No really, how *are* you? I'm asking twice to emphasise the breadth of my sincerity.

These are strange times, aren't they? I know I'm definitely feeling worse-for-wear. You might be able to tell that from my laid-back apparel, and from the fact I'm holding a mug. It's empty, of course, but doesn't it make you feel warm just to imagine it? Like I'm in your house *right now* having a friendly little chat? I'm not really in your house. In fact, I don't really exist at all! I'm just a smiling illusion created to demonstrate that I'm a real person from a real company that *cares*. Doesn't it feel like I care? Close your eyes. Listen. Shhhhhhh. Have you noticed my down-to-earth, regional accent? I'm one of you. I understand.

Now, there is the small matter of not knowing exactly who *you* are. After all, you could be

anyone! Never mind. Here's a montage of vari-
ously diverse families enjoying their limited time
together over a series of electronic devices. You
might see yourself in one of these faces. Here
we are laughing at the dinner table. Here I am
tucking you into bed. Here we are sharing a forehead kiss. But wait, can you hear that? It's the
sound of a classic rock-song from the 80s, except
now it's being covered by a whispery soprano
sounding somewhat like a ghost. Listen to the
piano's tinkle. Doesn't the tinkle soothe you? We
borrowed it from a variety show; they used it for
a sentimental montage after publicly mocking the
mentally ill.

I can see I still haven't convinced you. Perhaps
it will help if I introduce some rhyming couplets?

This is for the dreamers,
The overachievers,
The essential workers,
The booty-twerkers,
The fighters,
The up-all-nighters,
The washer-uppers,
The 'Fancy a cuppers?'

Those who like being listed *and* anally fisted
by multi-millionaire corporations abusing their
staff in the middle of an international pandemic
still hoping to manipulate the public by pretending to be a real person with genuine thoughts
and feelings who *cares.* Doesn't it feel like I care?

I'm so sorry. We seem to have gotten off track. Still, don't forget, we're here for you. Now, more than ever, you can rely on us.

Nunca Más

The church bells chimed, a deep vibrato, signalling a quarter to the hour. It was nearing midnight, and I could not have been more prepared. Rain pounded heavy on the skylight, but the rest was all in silence. My room was dimmed. The only means of viewing my surroundings was through candle and lamplight. This cinnamon scent pleasantly intermingled with that of my clean bed sheets. Today I'd gotten around to all those pernickety errands that often elude us for longer than they should, and with my head against my soft, clean pillow I was comforted by the lemony, soapy scent of Lenor. I rested, a paperback between my fingers, with every intention of finishing the story, but alas, my eyelids drooped, and the words swam in front of me in such a way that signalled any reading done would have to be repeated. I placed the book aside, yawning, and went to flick off the lamp beside me.

And I had sworn the skylight had been closed due to the rain, and the doors were all locked safely. However, if this were the case then no stranger could possibly have entered my dwelling place (unless it was the cat, perhaps? But no, she rested still, curled up beside my feet). Yet suddenly I became aware of a fluttering sound above me. A deep emerald shape swooped before me, extinguishing the candle in its wake. At first, it seemed like a blur of feathers and claws, before it settled down, its talons digging into the doorframe above, staring at me with eyes as wide as clock faces, opening its grotesque orange beak:

"Hola," cawed the intruder.

"Hola," I responded, conscious of my shaking breath, "El búho de Duolingo."

It was clear that I was in no position to continue much of an entertaining conversation, wrapped up in fresh sheets and warm pyjamas, pleasantly safe indoors on this dark and stormy night. Despite my usually polite and amiable nature, I felt a stab of dread as the bird stared down at me, contempt apparent in its circular, boring eyes.

"Qué tal?" I attempted.

In response, the owl simply laughed, as mockingly as one can laugh when burdened with a beak. It responded in its unnecessarily facetious tone.

"¿Qué tal? Bueno… a ver. Estoy enojado contigo, mi amor."

"Pero… ¿Por qué?" I stuttered helplessly.

"Sabes por qué," it scoffed, mercilessly.

I took a deep sigh. Truly, I had known this day would come. "Si. Lo sé."

"Olvidaste tu lección de español."

"Lo sé."

"Y por qué?"

"Yo estaba ocupada, yo…"

"Mentirosa!"

Tears filled up my eyes, the hot shame of all that I had promised, and failed, overwhelming me. The all-knowing eyes of Duolingo bore into my heart, and I clutched my chest in agony.

"I'll do it now. I still have fifteen minutes. I…"

"En Español," quoth the búho, "por favor."

"¡Ya tengo quince minutos! Lo puedo…"

But alas, the church bells did then ring, one dong after another, vibrating through the rain a dozen times. Lightning flashed, and I caught a glimpse of electric blue, as though gods were warning me of what was now to come. The rain continued, unrelenting. My cat stretched out a paw, unconscious of the certain terror that was sure to follow.

"No…" I gasped in agony.

"Es verdad," the owl confirmed. "Me has fallado."

"No!" I cried. "Please!"

Quoth the búho: "¡Por favor! Y ahora sabes las consecuencias…"

"Mi alma, y las vidas de mi familia. Pero, soy una buena persona. No puedo tener la sangre de mi familia en los manos."

The owl stopped me in my tracks with the turning of its head, 360 degrees anticlockwise, and again I felt the shiver of dread arising from the helplessness of my situation, and the inevitable carnage that was to follow.

"Pobre..." tutted the owl. "Pobre. Quieres decir... **LAS** manos."

I knew then that all was lost, and my fate was fully sealed. Now, all I could do was watch as those I loved were taken from me, brutally, to feed the bloodlust of this shiny, opal demon with an unquenchable thirst for the ignorance of innocents. I curled up on myself within those bedsheets, and I sobbed. The candle had been blown out by the swooping of his wings, but still I felt the tingling of Lenor fabric softener in my nostrils, the only comfort I had left in what would soon become a cold and heartless world.

To this day, the bird still haunts me. Its shadow left under my eyes and in the hollows of my cheeks. I no longer have the strength to eat, and wine tastes bitter on my tongue as I recall the vineyards of La Rioja and my greatest mistake. Rest is impossible. Siestas and fiestas are a thing of a bygone era, a time when I remember hope and joy, where the trees swayed in the breeze, and fresh bed sheets lulled me into gorgeous, deep unconsciousness. But now the owl has taken everything. I have no happiness, no loved ones to appeal to. In desperation, I can only beg for relief from this servitude, but the round eyes are so unforgiving. They show no mercy. And so I

must collapse upon this rotten bedroom floor and
futilely ask for an end to this unceasing madness.
Please, an ending. Por favor.

Peach

Anushka sips green tea flavoured with hints of peach and lemon, a combination intended to detoxify, but Anu tastes nothing, instead tongueing the burnt patch of skin on the roof of her mouth. Anu always packs her own tea bags. Her handbag is organised with an abundance of money-saving essentials: teabags, reusable thermos, Vaseline, paperclips, fluffy ear-warmers, and today, a thick, black mass of hair, limp and lifeless, buried inside.

Anu is waiting for her office to open so she can get on with her day translating ingredient listings. She doesn't need to be in until nine, really, and right now it's only 8:15, but things at home have been so tense she's been leaving earlier and earlier just to get some peace of mind. Now, she sits outside the café watching the building opposite, cradling her tea and waiting for the caretaker to arrive.

She needn't have bothered rising early. Her flatmate Peach is lazy, never gets up until midday even on weekdays, which Anu resents. Her company pays her a sizable salary to work from home, so Peach spends her mornings dossing about in harem pants, drinking coffee and (over)watering the plants. In the afternoon, she sits with her laptop in front of the telly, messing about with Photoshop, or whatever it is she does.

She'd explained it to Anu once before:

"You ever seen that video where they take posh snobs to an art gallery and ask them what they think of the paintings, and they all say they're, like, super profound and wonderful, and then they reveal that, actually, it's just mass-produced crap from IKEA?"

"No." Anu had frowned, looking down at her list of interview questions and wondering what this had to do with her financial situation.

"Oh. Well, I'm the creator of the mass-produced crap from IKEA."

Peach had laughed then, a huge guffaw, and Anu noticed how nice and white her teeth looked in her face. Peach was half-German, half-Indian, which had initially excited Anu until she learned that Peach was "shite at all languages" since she'd grown up on a council estate in Leeds.

"I'm only fluent in Northern, mate," she'd said.

Anu tried not to look disappointed. Her master's degree had been in linguistics, and she was fluent in Russian, Polish, French, German, and English. Translating documents for a food-manufacturing company wasn't her dream, but the pay was good, and any excess money she had could be spent on books. Classic literature was Anu's vice. She bought the best books she could get her hands on, all in the original language so that she could read them as the author intended. Hardback gems painted the shelves like a rainbow in her bright, white apartment. Peach had said that was one of the reasons she'd wanted to move in.

"I can pretend the books are mine and use my 'culture' to get laid, innit." Peach had laughed then too.

Anu didn't really want a new flatmate, but she couldn't afford the place by herself, and since Higgs had unceremoniously left her, she needed an alternative. Well, he hadn't so much left her as she'd thrown him out after a row, but that was never intended to be permanent as he should have well known. Usually after one of their fights, he'd come back with a houseplant (she'd always hated bunches of flowers, dying, wilting, hacked off at the root), and she'd let him back inside. The last time, however, he simply hadn't come back. She'd told him to go, stomped around the place in a huff, but by the time she'd had a long, relaxing bubble bath and read a little Dostoyevsky (beautiful copy, serrated pages, lavender paperback, all in the original Russian), she'd forgiven him. When she rang his mobile, it went to voicemail. When he finally did pick up, it was to arrange collecting his things. The bills and rent were already in her name, so all it took for him to leave was a brief cancellation of his standing order to her account. Online banking. One click. Anu was left to fend for herself. So she found Peach.

Anu decided this girl would be *fine* to move in. Not ideal. Just fine. Practically nobody her own age could afford rent in the city, and at least a woman would leave less stubble in the sink.

It was obvious the arrangement wouldn't work after around four or five days. The coffee cups by the sink and the curry boxes dripping yellow liquid in the fridge were repulsive. When Peach cooked, she always burned something, and the stink lingered for hours. Her hair was the worst part. Those long, thick strands gathered in the plughole, turning grey and slimy before Anu (and it *was* always Anu) pulled them out with the marigolds hanging loosely off her fingers. Peach styled her hair in front of the television at night, unwrapping her messy bun and holding the waist-length swath in one hand as she brushed it, leaving her tangles on the floor. Anu even saw her pull the loose strands from her shoulders and flick them directly onto the carpet, as though it didn't matter, as though Peach ever vacuumed. These things Anu initially accepted with a calm exhale and a clenched jaw. After all, Higgs hasn't been much better, although he followed her diet, and he'd adopted a sensible crew cut in their most recent years together, a vast improvement on the scruffy, seventies-footballer thing he'd had when they'd first met. But Anu understood, as someone who knew few people and liked fewer, that being around things you didn't enjoy was a necessary evil in this world. She gritted her teeth and carried on.

About three weeks into their arrangement, Anu awoke at 2 a.m. with cramps. Painful, sleepless nights tended to happen the first and second day of each cycle: the sharp back stab, the low mood, the tender triangle breasts that felt foreign and strange to her, all of it created a foulness that stopped her from sleeping. Her sleeplessness fed into her anxiety when she thought about how she'd have to wake up for work soon (there were always going to be documents to translate), and the more she thought about it, the more every second felt like doom. She forced herself up to get Nurofen.

Anu still wasn't used to Peach's odd hours, and she scowled when she saw the blue glow beneath the bedroom door which meant her tacky fairy-lights were still turned on. The buzz of her epilator (she needed it for all that *hair*) was going strong. Anu resented that Peach probably didn't know or care about the time. She could relax at 2 a.m. without thinking about getting up. While it wasn't *technically* her fault that Anu was awake, Anu felt it very well could have been. She planned to knock on the door and ask her to turn it down, to tell her, with a practised sigh, "I'm sorry to be rude, but the buzz is just constant. Could you sort your legs out another time?" But when she got close to the door, she realised she heard something else, some slight gasping as though Peach was out of breath. Was she crying? She leant closer, wondering whether to knock and see if she was okay, knowing that if she did that she'd have to drop her veil of self-righteousness, and then Anu realised that what she heard wasn't crying but moaning.

It clicked. After a few seconds, she managed to get a grip and make it back into her bedroom, the water and Nurofen left forgotten on the kitchen counter. She tossed and turned for hours, the cramps worsening as she pictured her forgotten Nurofen, which she knew would be too awkward to retrieve.

Anu thought about calling in sick the next day, but she would have been stuck in the house with Peach anyway, so she forced herself into the office. After a full day's work, all she wanted was to collapse on the sofa and relax when she got home, but of course, that couldn't happen. Peach was there (wasn't she always?), and now she had her friend Katie with her. They were lying on each other, stretched out on the sofa, Peach's head resting on Katie's chest as they watched the telly, a crumpled mess of open crisp packets on the table next to them. Anu knew they were there before she'd taken off her shoes, heard Katie's whining voice from the hallway: "Urgh, mate, have you just farted on me?" and grimaced.

She had to walk through the living room to get to her bedroom.

"Hiya," Peach said, not looking away from the screen as Anu entered the main space.

"Hi," Anu replied, trying to keep all emotion out of her voice.

"Whoa! What's up with you? You look like shite warmed-up," Peach said, to which Katie giggled inanely, and Anu wondered how someone so rude could have so many friends.

"I didn't sleep."

"Aw, bless. Insomnia's the worst, innit?" Peach sounded almost genuine. Katie was mute, her eyes glued to the TV, waiting for Anu to walk on through so they could carry on their regular conversation. The thought, however, of going to her room to be trapped there, a prisoner in her own home, didn't particularly appeal to Anu. She decided to give Peach a taste of her own medicine.

"Yes. I was up all night. You must have been up late too. Were you epilating your legs last night? Around 2:30?"

"Um… no?" Peach ran a hand over her shins. "Still a hairy bitch. Why?"

"Oh that's so strange. I thought I could hear something … vibrating." Anu smirked, waiting for the realisation to drop.

"At 2:30 a.m.?"

"Yes. Something loudly *vibrating* in the middle of the night."

Katie and Peach looked at each other, and Katie sucked her lips in, trying not to laugh.

"Um, yeah," Peach began, "that was probably my vibrator, pal. Sorry."

Katie's laughter spurted out like a leak, and Peach started guffawing too. Anu could only stare, crestfallen as she realised she was the only one in the room who felt embarrassed. Somehow, the joke had ended up being on her.

"I mean, do you want me to keep it down, or…?" Peach asked, this time with no hint of genuity.

"No," Anu said, too quickly. "It's fine."

With her embarrassing attempt at a telling off finished, Anu headed to her room. She was too flustered to even make an excuse. Just before she'd closed the door to her bedroom, she heard Katie stage-whisper: "Mate, what the fuck?"

Anu slammed the door behind her.

Of course, it was too much to expect that Peach's constant stream of visitors could at least stick to the human variety.

"Why call it Sandy? Sandy suggests blonde," Anu had said.

"Yeah, but this is Sandi with an 'I,' like Sandi Toksvig from QI. You like all that Russian shit, and the house could use some more badass, lesbian energy, you know?"

Anu took a deep breath. "I think if you wanted to name a dog Sandy, you should have gotten a blonde dog."

Peach laughed. "Alright mate, next time the shelter says they're putting a dog down, I'll make sure it's a blonde one, yeah?"

Peach had technically asked permission to get a puppy but had done so in such a way that Anu knew she'd look like a monster if she declined. She asked in front of a group of friends (everywhere Peach went, she was surrounded by groups of friends), and when Anu stiffly responded: "I have no issue, but the landlord will never allow it," Peach had the WhatsApp conversation with the landlord up and ready to go. Anu scrolled through the messages, littered with laughing emojis and heart eyes. Clearly, Peach had charmed Gerado. Above the messages where she'd asked for a puppy, she'd taken a selfie next to the (no longer leaky) bathroom tap, a toolbox in the background captioned "Girl Boss Plumber Bitch." Gerado had responded with a laughing face and this message: "Congratulations, my favourite tenant! Much cheaper than a plumber, no?"

Anu had thought her relationship with their landlord was friendly. He let her practise Italian with him. She'd even bonded with him over her gorgeous, hot-red copy of Dante's *Inferno*. Now she could see that their relationship was civil at best.

"Okay fine," Anu said. "Get a dog."

Peach squealed like a kettle when she hugged her.

There were times when Anu thought about wringing Sandy's neck, but Anu was the only one who ever cleaned up after the animal, and so it saw her as something of an owner. When those little black paws would clamber up her legs, Anu knew she didn't have it in her to murder an animal, even a disgusting sickbag like this one. Peach's neck, on the other hand, she could have wrung with joy.

The days blurred. Dog shit, puddles on the kitchen floor, one tiny tin bowl for meat, another for biscuits, one thousand pictures of Peach and Sandy on Instagram.

"Three months with <3 Sandi <3."

The picture showed Sandy on Peach's lap, Peach's thick hair braided as she tilted her head to the side, her wide, brown eyes lined with kohl, lids glittering. Sandy had her tongue out, her little spaniel ears curled in a way that could have made them twins. That picture alone got 400 likes. Peach drew pictures inspired by the animal, charcoal on large sheets of A3 paper which stained Anu's wooden coffee table. She bluetacked them to the living room walls and ruined the paint.

Coming home from work meant coming home to the smell of dog food. When Anu got up at night to grab more water and Nurofen, she'd inevitably step in the little tin bowls. Not that the food always stayed in its designated areas. Sandy developed the charming habit of throwing up whatever she'd eat, always so excited at the prospect of food that she couldn't keep it down. Anu had had her own flirtings with bulimia in the past, but Sandy really was the expert. The carpet now had splotches of dark where the scrubbing up from "accidents" hadn't truly worked, and its once cream-colour was now murky with the hairs that sprinkled the floor like black ice.

Anu wasn't sleeping. She was biting her knuckles again. Peach feigned a willingness at helping with the cleaning.

"Just leave it. I'll do it in the morning," she'd shout from the living room sofa as Anu forced herself to do the washing up, piles of mugs all stained coffee-brown with bitty grains of sugar up the side. Anu ignored these shouts. She knew well enough that Peach's mornings were the afternoon to everyone else.

And the buzzing didn't stop. At night time, Anu would hear it going incessantly until the final sharp little squeak would let her know that things were done, but even then, she couldn't truly rest. She would lean her forehead against Peach's door, daring her to open it so she could explain that she'd been woken up, once again. That never happened. Apparently, Peach just went straight back to sleep. It made Anu wonder if she ever washed her hands.

In the morning, before stopping by the café for hot water, before sitting outside to wait for the caretaker, before stoically ignoring the frantic ringing in her handbag as Peach grew more and more incensed, Anu had left early for work. She hadn't slept, and when she forced herself out of bed and into the kitchen, she stepped directly onto one of Sandy's fur-balls.

Contrary to popular belief, it isn't just cats that get fur-balls. Anu had found out quite awfully that dogs got them too. In cartoons, fur-balls were always like tumbleweeds, neat little balls rolling along the ground. Sandy's fur-balls were not like that. They were wet and slimy and black with all the hair, not just its own but Peach's too, which presumably the dog had swallowed as it snuggled up to her at night or inhaled as it dug up the carpet or licked up from the bathroom sink as it tried to get the drops of water (that faucet fix Peach did proved useless in the end), and Anu felt like screaming. Perhaps if she had screamed, things would have been better. Peach would have woken up. They would have had a row. Perhaps it would be like with Higgs; Peach would leave and then come back with a houseplant and an apology. But Anu's shouting days were over. Instead, she grabbed the miniature shears from the kitchen drawer and snuck into Peach's room.

Peach, naturally, stayed asleep. Her room smelt of farts and weed. Sandy, next to her on the pillow, wasn't such a heavy sleeper. It looked at Anu with wide, brown eyes beneath its curly black eyebrows. It was a good job that Anu so often looked after the animal because it didn't growl or whine when she picked it up from the pillow.

Now that tangled black mass of hair lies in her handbag. It seems a lot smaller there than it did on the pillow. Anu's phone vibrates again, this time not a ring, but a double buzz which lets her know that Peach had switched to text. Anu sighs, placing down her thermos. Would all her mornings be disturbed by Peach's excessive vibrating?

You bitch, you bitch, you bitch!!!

I'm calling the police.

This is technically assault.

I'm gonna fucking kill you. You'll rue the day you were born.

Anu scrolls through these messages with cold indifference. She supposes she'll have to find a new flatmate. A shame. She'd almost miss the dog.

The caretaker drives up in their filthy sedan, and Anu smiles, gathering her things. She checks her handbag just to be sure she had everything: wallet, phone, keys, teabags, earmuffs, and Peach's hacked off ponytail, smaller now, looking almost impotent in its tangled, messy state. She puts her phone on silent. Her work day is beginning, and for the first time in a while, she feels at peace.

Pillow Talk

Sunday morning and far too late to still be in bed. The shut curtains tainted the room a cosy pink. She could hear rain plinking on the windows, tricking her into feeling warm enough not to worry about the twisted sheets, the gathering of mess: wine-glasses, underwear, used tissues, ripped packets… a veritable Emin display of idleness. She knew that if someone were to walk in, the room would smell like unwashed bodies.

She'd both slept and not slept, dozing on and off for hours. Behind her, he'd been the same. She could tell this from the snuffling half-kisses on her crown, the infrequent toilet trips, the vague understanding in her semi-conscious state that pillows and blankets were being rearranged around her. Now though, he was dead asleep. His black stubble framed his jaw, his eyelashes girlishly long. She didn't want to kiss him, but she wanted him to leave, so she stroked her lips against his, hoping it would make him stir.

"Morning," he muttered, eyes still closed.

"Hi," she replied. *Please wake up. I only have half the day left, and I need to do laundry and clean my apartment and shower, and it's hard to do that with you here because I need to be human, not angelic, and I'm not sure we're ready for that kind of reality yet.*

It didn't work. His eyes remained closed. Hers were open, intrigued by his prettiness, the vacant nature of his lineless face. His mouth was slightly open, inhaling and exhaling with the tiniest effort. To kiss him again would look childish.

Her skin erupted into goosebumps when she peeled back the bedsheets. She scavenged around on the floor for clothes that she could step into easily, but every sound made her cringe. She was an elephant stomping around, jangling keys in pockets, letting buttons hit the hardwood floor, and she knew that her ex-partners were right in that she *was* annoying. She hoped he didn't think her attempt at dressing was a means of demanding his attention, but deep down, she knew he would and resented it. His attention was the last thing she wanted.

"Is everything alright?" he asked.

"Yeah, fine, I'm just going to brush my teeth." *And wash my face and brush my hair and maybe shit because I'm feeling bloated from the wine, and I can spray on some deodorant and remove my crusty mascara and start to look presentable...*

"No, come back here." He playfully pulled her arm, and she submitted, turning away from him to keep her morning breath out of his face. She let her body fold into his, twinned foetal positions.

"Okay, a few more minutes." *I wonder how long this will take,* but soon, against her better judgement, she was drifting off again. Even in her state of hungover discomfort, it was warm and soft enough that dozing turned to sleeping, and she had vivid dreams about swimming in a giant vat of vomit.

She was nice to look at. Her profile was soft with its small nose and chin, the sort of defined jaw that told him she wore a retainer as an adolescent. His arm was starting to go dead, but he didn't want to wake her by cruelly yanking it away. Instead, he stroked her hair behind her ear and kissed her cheek, hoping she would rouse. She stayed sleeping. He kissed her harder and moved down to her neck and sucked beneath her ear, and when she moaned in confusion, he rose up against her.

"Oh, hi," she said, smiling. *Should I tell him that I don't like to wake up in this way because I often dream of swimming in a giant vat of vomit?*

"Hey," he gasped.

"So, you're awake now?" *I hope he finds this playfulness coy and not embarrassing.*

"Aha, yeah." He reached down, gently parting her legs. The rain was hammering down now, and he kissed her cheek, her neck. She kept her mouth closed, pressed her face into the pillow, arched her back to suggest a more feminine curve than was really there. She liked this position best because there wasn't much cardio required, and yet it wasn't Missionary Position which, although enjoyable, had connotations of dull, middle-aged repression. It felt good to have his large hands on her hips pulling her towards him. She thought he must be agonised that there wasn't more of her to push himself into. He was getting close. When he started slowing down, it bothered her. She was still sore from yesterday, and she didn't want this to go on forever when she still hadn't showered, still hadn't brushed her teeth, still hadn't…

"Baby, faster." *Please, so I can get on with my day.*

"But I'm so close."

She asked him to cum for her in the high-pitched whine she knew appealed to many men, of which she hoped he was one.

"Oh God," he moaned.

That little death, the tiny kamikaze, the final pop at the end of the firework display.

"Wow," she feigned breathlessness, "that was amazing." *I can't forget my pill again.*

As he removed himself, she felt his spunk drip down her thighs, and it pleased her. Perhaps it was only pleasant *because* it was disgusting, because if this was on her leg in clear daylight or underneath a trouser suit at the office, people would recoil, and that was fascinating to her. Sometimes she liked to be called a whore in bed. It added to the sense that this was sordid as pure hell, and she preferred that. People who whispered in her ear as they told her she was beautiful made her want to grate her skin off where they'd touched her.

"Now, I really need a shower." She laughed. *If I piss now, I'll reduce the risk of urinary tract infections.*

"I'll come join you in a sec," he said.

"Sure." *Better not take that shit then.*

When pissing, she realised her body smelt different post-coitus. Her vagina was usually sweet and coppery, but now it was sour. She hoped her body-wash might help but knew from experience that it rarely did.

As she lathered herself up in the shower, she found that she wanted to sing but didn't know what kind of music would give off the right impression. She wanted to scream clean, bohemian yet uncontentious. She heard the bathroom door shut as he entered. He opened the shower door, letting in a flood of cold air, and she covered herself with her arms, feeling more self-conscious being naked here than she did in the bedroom. The light emphasised every blackhead and stray hair. He leant forward to kiss her, his hair dampened by the shower's spray. She leant forward too, placed her too-wet arm around his neck. She'd brushed her teeth already, thankfully. He hadn't, but that hardly mattered.

"I'll probably head off now," he said. A sudden stomach jab.

"Oh. Is everything okay?"

"Yeah, yeah, fine, I've just got stuff to be getting on with."

Immediately, she thought of other women, but then why would that matter? Why was jealousy her instinctual reaction towards any new man who stumbled across her path?

"Do you want me to show you out?" *Don't leave now, please. Don't leave me here.*

"No, I'm good. See you around."

While she washed her hair, she agonised over what she could have done to repel him. Did she come across too cold? Too desperate? Was the morning sex bad, did he smell her terrible breath, did he feel the stubble on her shins where the cold had air lifted up the miniscule hairs for a moment? She wondered if getting in the shower had made her seem uptight, whether he somehow knew that she dreamt of vomit and analysed the smells of her own body. It didn't matter. Somehow, she'd fucked it.

Today was a day for comfortable cotton underwear. She put on jeans and a button up shirt, no bra, trying to feel clean and free. Last night's mesh of cut up cloth and string was limp on the floor, stinking of cigarettes and aniseed. She sipped her cup of coffee, knowing it was far too late in the day for a first cup of coffee, remade her bed, and opened the curtains. The rain had stopped, but the sky was still a brutal, slate grey. The morning's misery was present in the puddles filled with soggy leaves.

Last night was the kind of thing she was supposed to enjoy. Rashly, she decided that she would allow this man to intrude on her life indefinitely, at least until he got bored, and then when she was really invested, she would let him break her heart. She knew that it would hurt, but this plan of action always made the most sense to her. After all, she already knew the shapes of him. She already knew what he felt like.

Outside, a man dragged his crying child along by the arm, frustrated by her tears. The little girl's face was red enough to indicate genuine distress. She didn't want to move forward, and when her father jerked her arm, she fell on the concrete and scraped her knee. Of course, then the crying turned to screams, and the father shouted down at her, exasperated: "Walk properly, then!"

The child stood and started to follow, but still she screamed, a hole in her white woollen tights the size of a five-penny piece, a little red pocket visible beneath the tear.

Poor kid. The woman finished the dregs of her coffee. *She'll learn eventually just to go along with it all.*

The Popular Virgin Blood Misconception

There's something magical about a fold-down ladder coming down in three solid clunks, landing with a muted thud on carpeted floor. A bat should've flown out the hole, but it didn't. There were spider webs on the rungs, though. I liked that. It was the kind of aesthetic I would expect from a rickety ceiling ladder, and it's fun when things go to plan.

I doubted this would go to plan for the boys, though. Currently, they were taking me upstairs with a switchblade against my back, not that they truly needed it. I would've gone with them willingly, and anyway, they clearly didn't expect me to put up a fight. Spinella had taught me how to read auras. She swore it was magic, but it sounded more like common sense to me. I knew they didn't expect me to put up a fight because they sounded too smug. They weren't as nervous as I might have expected. Two of them, the side-kicks I'll call them, were sweating, clearly anxious about getting caught, although shamefully *not* anxious about the state of their immortal souls. The other one, the leader with the switchblade, wasn't shaking in the slightest. His breathing was calm. He seemed excited but not nervous. A genuine psychopath. What a delight!

"Upstairs," he ordered.

Perhaps I should have whimpered or moaned something along the lines of: "Oh, whatever you do, please don't hurt me," but I didn't. Spinella would have enjoyed a melodramatic reaction, but I don't think it would have been possible for me to keep a straight face. So I climbed. I wondered if they were looking up the very short skirt of my cheerleader uniform; if this was a film, that's where the camera would have lingered (they sure do love to relish in our bodies, don't they?). The boys followed up after me, and with the switchblade lowered for a second, I was able to take in the attic.

It was perfect. The light was ideal for a séance. There was only one small window covered in moss, and light trickled through just enough to symbolise hope. The boxes (of… what? Old family photo albums? Baby clothes?) were covered with beige dust-cloths anyway, the kind of dust-cloths you'd wrap a body in before throwing it in a canal. I wished I could have shown Spinella. She would have set up an altar and hot-boxed the room with her incense, but I didn't have a camera. With svelte thinking, the boys had swooped on me after practice when I had nothing but myself and my crisp, white uniform with its cherry red numbers and hems. At least my shoes were good for running. At least I'd tied my hair.

"Get on the fucking floor," the leader said, and my musing was brought to an abrupt finish. I knelt gently on the creaking, wooden ground and waited patiently. Already, I was feeling quite excited. Sidekick #1, his glasses misting up beneath his hockey mask, was drawing a pentagram on the floor with blackboard chalk. "No, over here." The leader jangled the chains to get my attention.

Ah! How could I not have noticed the manacles? They were attached to the wall in a Sadeian sex-dungeon manner. A true aesthetic. Not that I really saw the appeal in the *practical* side of sex dungeons. Famously, I had a reputation for being an awful prude, and it was fairly earned: purity ring, "just-say-no" t-shirt—I even wore a gentle crucifix around my neck which fell so beautifully against my cleavage that I barely minded the staring. When I was first alone with Spinella and she saw that cross, she flicked it upside down with her pierced tongue and made me promise that I'd never forget how good it looked when sat correctly. I laughed at her faux seriousness. With her black hair and eyeliner, she always wanted to come across so morbid, but it was all just too much fun!

The boy clamped me in place so that my arms were held above me, and I shifted so that my legs stretched out in front. I caught a flicker of suspicion through the eyeholes of his hockey mask and wondered why before I realised I hadn't uttered a word of complaint so far and probably looked far calmer than I should have done.

"Oh, please don't hurt me," I wailed quickly. He snorted and stood up.

Now, despite the intention of anonymity, I knew exactly who these three kidnappers were. Who didn't? Or more accurately, who wouldn't have predicted them? It was the skinny boy with the mousy brown hair and chin acne who got caught shooting nerf guns up trees to hurt the squirrels and his two best friends (one bespectacled redhead with halitosis, and one overweight boy, and gosh in high-school if you were overweight, wasn't that really all that mattered?). The three of them sat together in the cafeteria laughing at ISIS beheading videos. They were bullied, of course. They always smelled a little bit of weed and a lot of BO. They would have gotten turned on by the idea of killing me, I had no doubt about it.

The overweight boy, very obviously still him even in his hockey mask, was now lighting black candles. He placed them in a circle around the pentagram. They gently rang the bell.

"Oh Satan, we thank you for appearing to us and showing us the way. We pray that you will hear our demands."

Demands?! Oh dear. These boys were far too entitled to really indulge in this kind of spiritual performance.

"We offer to you these sacrifices…"

One dead pigeon, already filled with maggots, a doll stuck full of pins, a folded piece of paper, no doubt filled with horrific descriptions of the injuries they would like to inflict on me.

"Hail Satan," said the leader.

"Hail Satan," mimicked the other two.

"And now for the most important part. The blood of a virgin." He turned to face me. "You know what's coming, don't you, Little Miss Abstinence?"

I managed a sad smile. "You don't have to kill me. If you let me go, I promise I won't tell."

I couldn't see his mouth, but I'm sure he was grinning. "Too late for all that now."

He crouched in front of me, switchblade popped open. He looked carefully from the top of my face to the bottom, left to right, taking it all in as though surveying a wall for where to best hang a hook. The cut hurt. I won't deny that. Clearly, he'd chosen my cheek because he was angry at my beauty (I know we girls shouldn't admit it, but must I pretend to be blind?). The good part was, I didn't have to put on a brave face. In fact, the more pathetic I acted, the more convincing the whole thing would be. At least now, after being sliced, I was angry. That energy was good. It meant it would be easier to channel Him through me when the time came.

The drops of my blood fell into a skull-shaped vial, and he took it over to the pentagram.

"Our Lord Satan, please take this mortal sacrifice, and ensure revenge will be mine."

Revenge for what? I wondered. Life? Existence in general? The decline in white, male superiority? Ah well, it hardly mattered in the end. At least these boys were slightly more creative than your average school shooter.

"So it is done." The leader spoke loudly, dripping my blood on top of the rotting pigeon.

"So it is done," the side-kicks murmured after.

There was a pause of perhaps a minute, if that. I found their impatience staggering.

"So, it *is* done, right?" the red-headed side-kick asked. "Like… how do we know it worked?"

"I feel different. Don't you feel different?" the overweight boy said.

"He will reveal it to us when the time is right," the leader responded smugly.

"Oh, I don't think so," I interjected. I could feel His power running through me now. They had summoned Him for a ritual they'd performed incorrectly, and He was angry. That was the problem with worshipping a creature like Satan—there was always that fiery temper to contend with. It was something you grew fond of over time. I felt fond of it now, as it filled me from the stomach upwards, my face pleasantly warm and tingling. He was here.

The leader snorted.

"The fuck are you talking about?"

"Well, the ritual." I smiled. "You got the ingredients wrong."

"Shit," said the overweight boy. "Well, we can do it again, right?"

"I can't snap another pigeon neck," the redhead continued. "I only managed to do this one because Fluffy had already got to it, but it was still gross."

"Relax," the leader said. "She's making things up. She knows we're going to kill her and she's trying to get out of it." He moved so that he could squat down in front of me. He lifted up his mask. To my complete lack of surprise, it was precisely who I knew it was. There was his mousy brown fringe, his long nose, the mole on his cheek I couldn't stand to look at. It was brave, though. If he was showing me his face, he really did mean to kill me. "I'm sorry, Princess. It's too late. The only ingredient that matters is the virgin blood, and if that cut's not enough, then we can just slit your throat on the pentagram. So you see? It's no problem. We were going to do it anyway."

"Yes, you're right." I sighed. "The virgin blood is the most important. It's just a shame you got the blood part wrong."

The overweight boy threw down their spellbook. "I knew it! I fucking knew it."

"She's not a virgin?" asked the redhead.

"Oh, what does that even mean?" I scoffed. "Have I been penetrated? Fucked? Has a penis successfully broken my hymen? No. So, why not? You can call me a virgin if you're into that kind of thing. The problem is it's not a virgin cheerleader you need. It's virgin *blood*."

"What does that even mean?" the leader said, and I knew I had his attention, then, because the smirk was slipping.

"It's actually a common misconception. The blood can't have been used in a ritual for Him before. It has to be pure. Untainted. Virginal, if you will."

"Oh right. And your blood has been used in a satanic ritual before, has it?"

At that point, He broke the manacles. Well, I suppose I did it really. My bones felt like steel, and I bashed through the metal. I stood up, and my legs were sore from sitting on the floor. I stamped out the pins and needles and stretched, my exposed stomach arching like a cat's.

"That's much better." I yawned. "I was getting so stiff down there."

The boys were looking at me aghast. I grinned. I knew how I appeared to them. My short skirt, my leg pulled into a quad stretch, one hand on my hip. I shook my ponytail and laughed at their terrified faces. Of course, I was extra giddy because of Him. When He enters you, you feel strong as an ox and light as a feather and completely indestructible. Your veins feel electric. He was good to me because I was good to Him. Me and Spinella kept track of all the holidays. We prayed. We worshipped avidly. There was nothing but respect and awe towards our Father. The great one. Oh, how I loved Him.

"Now, as for whether my blood has been used in a ritual before, it has. More times than I can count, God, thousands. Not because I'm kidnapped a lot, of course. It's just that my mate Spinner, you know her, I'm sure? Well she is just *super* anaemic. I keep telling her to eat her greens but no… So, anyway I take one for the team, and it's a privilege, you know? You give yourself to Him, and He'll give himself to you, and He trusts you. He'll be there for you when it's dark. God, look at me! A sixteen-year-old girl and I'm not scared of anything anymore! For the price of willing devotion? A little bit of blood? A perfect trade off."

The boys stared at me dumbstruck.

"How did you get out?" the redhead said weakly. "James, is this a joke?"

"Oh no, trust me, he's no idea about anything." I laughed. "He came to Satan with *demands*. I mean, even with the right ingredients, it would have been a stretch. It's a shame. Spinner's great with stuff like this, bookish, she knows what she's doing and she could have helped you, but you had to just mess it up yourself, didn't you? Well, I admire your tenacity."

"Get the fuck down on the floor," the leader (well, should I keep calling him the leader when he's so evidently not in charge of anything?) said.

"Oh princess," I smiled, "it's too late for all that now."

When I lifted my arms, they dropped down like rag dolls. Their blood flowed like a river, although I couldn't see the incisions. It trickled down their ears, their noses. James' eyes cried red. He was choking, and white vomit was frothing in his mouth. What would they call this when they found them? An epileptic fit? Their faces were white already, and I knew the redhead was already dead (physically and spiritually, he was weak). I walked through their blood to reach the bell, my tennis shoes picking up the red, splashing through like rain puddles. It rang daintily in the air. Three virgins. So much blood. I could already feel Him praising me.

"So," I shouted jubilantly, "it is done!"

And suddenly there was the sound of a gunshot. Brains hit the wall. The blood spurted neatly, and as I opened my eyes, the river had gone. Instead, I saw three bodies. There were three, neat little bullet holes, three messy little heads. The exit wounds were clean. A gun rested in James' hand, black and crooked. Of course, He was so clever. Everyone would believe a suicide pact about this ghastly lot.

I caught a glimpse of myself in the mossy window. The night had turned black, and I could see myself clearly with the candle light. My face was badly cut. I tutted. Hopefully, Spinella could fix it. She was a dab-hand with the ointments. I climbed back down the attic ladder, almost slipping from the blood. My shoes would need a wash too. I'd have to dry them out in the sun. The problem with a white uniform is that the stains are just hellish to deal with.

Shitmix

He was in a band called Anchors. They only ever played to around twenty people, but they always had parties on the beach after shows. Johnny would scream as he paced around the stage, hitting his head on the floor to show his passion and intensity. Girls like me but thinner, with blacker eyes, would nod along and call it poetry. Those girls were called the "coat-hangers." Their job was to hold the bags and jackets while the boys beat each other up until they bled. We liked it when they bled. Half the time, I couldn't understand a word those boys were singing, but I liked the bleeding all the same.

I stood at the front, and I jumped and jumped and jumped and burned calories. I avoided the punches as best I could, but sometimes they landed, and I would crumple. People always begrudgingly dragged me back up when I fell.

"No clit in the pit," they'd shout, but I think it secretly impressed them that I wasn't afraid to bleed too.

There was something so delicious then about the smell of sweat. At the afterparty, the ocean sweated with us, and we tasted the salty air, listened to the cawing of the seagulls. We drank Smirnoff straight from the bottle, shuddering as it went down. It was warmer that way, far better than mixing it in with soda water in sad little plastic cups. The wind had turned my sweat cold, so I wrapped my denim jacket tight around me, feeling grateful for the scratchy fabric on my skin.

When I felt alone, I drew happy faces in the sand. If asked, I planned to say I was making friends to smile up at me. I probably thought I was being ironic. No one paid any attention to my artistic rebellion. It was frustrating because I was deliberately *not* paying attention to the rest of the group in the hopes that they *might* pay attention to me. Instead, everyone watched Kayla, a coathanger with a purple undercut, as she tried to do a cartwheel, her stretched, flat stomach briefly exposed mid-air. I drew a sad face in the sand.

I felt Johnny sit next to me before I saw him, his stick-like silhouette in the corner of my eye. He was tall, obnoxiously so, and thin as a cheesestring, legs stretching out in front of him in skinny jeans.

"This is shitmix," he said to me. He held a bottle of what looked like dirty seawater. I must have grimaced because he added, "It looks bad, but there's magic in it."

"What is it?"

"Vodka, rum, bit of brandy… I think maybe some other stuff."

"Int that rank?"

"Yeah," he said, nodding. "Yeah, it's fucking awful."

He took a sip and passed it to me, and I almost didn't panic about the sugar content. As soon as I swallowed, I gagged. He was right; it was awful, like petrol laced with fizzy pop, but still I gulped down more.

As soon as Johnny pulled me in, the circle got wider to include me. Girls with nose-rings cuddled into each other affectionately. The band showed off their battle scars, piercings and tattoos. Everybody had tattoos. Johnny showed me his favourite: a skull on the sole of his foot.

"Why get it there? No one's going to see it," I said.

"It's not about seeing it," he told me. "The bottom of the foot is the most painful place to be tattooed. Every time I felt the needle, it was like a scalpel. I was scared I was going to pass out. Then I was even more scared that I wouldn't. It's a reminder, see? The pain is a reminder of death. Because death is coming, and I want to remember that every time I step."

"It still hurts?" I'd asked.

"No, but it's the memory. The memory of pain lasts a lifetime."

I nodded while he spoke and sipped on his shitmix. I remember thinking that he was the most intelligent man I'd met.

That wasn't the only time he used that speech. I heard him say it almost a year later to an angry girl in a punk band. No doubt he regaled the entire tattoo parlour with his philosophising during the entire, agonising process, if he could manage to speak. But to this day, he can't feel the damn tattoo. Why would you want to remember pain you needlessly inflicted on yourself for no reason other than the sake of remembering? Why am I remembering this now?

By the end of the night, the sky was tinted pink from light pollution, and I could feel his breath on my ear. I was frozen still, scared to knock him in case he moved away. Even now, I think of him as beautiful. His long hair and rosebud lips made me feel secure. His eyes were so blue they stood out in photos. I think that must have been why I loved him. Maybe it was projection, I don't know. I had muddy eyes and pimples. My hair was always matted together and tangled. I wasn't beautiful; I knew that. I was never going to be one of the girls with red lipstick and fishnets, I couldn't pull off a severe fringe, and I couldn't talk effortlessly with the girls who checked their noses in the bathroom mirror.

The lights from the hotels surrounding the beach created a dome of colour around us. The group was dwindling, and Johnny moved his head onto my lap.

"Is it cool if I sleep here?" he joked.

"Sure."

"Are you okay with me using you as a bed? Or do you only like guys using you *in* bed?"

"Watch it." I'd meant to laugh but hadn't. I must have been too nervous. "But maybe I should get the train home now, the last one."

"Oh, that train's long gone. Do you even know what time it is?"

Of course I knew the time. I'd been glancing at my watch all night, and Johnny was wrong because there was one last train. It was the last, last, last train at 1 a.m., deserted and empty aside from a few homeless people who used it as an opportunity to sleep on the seats. It always smelled like vomit, and I got an earful the next morning from my mum who always swore she'd been waiting up all night to hear the door close.

"You can stay at mine if you want to," he offered. And I did.

"Is this going to be a love story?" I asked him when we lay next to each other in bed, our faces perfectly aligned for a kiss. He laughed, a genuine laugh where his mouth stretched wide enough to show the cavities.

"I don't think love stories start with shitmix."

"They sure do end in them though," I said, and when he smiled half-heartedly, I realised that I hadn't made any sense.

I guess you would call it my virginity. I didn't even really know what virginity was. Girls in school bathrooms always talked about what "counted." Not the pretty fishnet girls; none of *them* were virgins that was for sure, and I doubted they cared what "counted." The ones who cared were the annoying lip-gloss girls who live in the school toilets applying make-up and vomiting into porcelain bowls. They all kind of agreed it was alright, not slaggy, as long as you loved them.

I did love Johnny, maybe. I loved the paleness of his skin and the blueness of his eyes. I loved the way his hip bones jutted out. I loved him because his beauty reflected well on me. It justified the way my stomach hung and the way my hair was never neat because if I had him then that meant I was okay. I'd asked him if this was a love story, and he had said it wasn't.

Course, they'd already told me all that at the clinic, but at the time, I didn't believe them. I tried to piece it together when the breakdown started. I wanted to blame him, to look deep inside myself and find that all of it stemmed right from his neglect of me, manically flicking through diaries to find the precise moment when he'd snapped my heart. But I searched for emotion and found only diet plans. I remember writing them down, and I remember following them, but I don't remember it happening so intensely. When Johnny left me for another girl, I blamed myself. I'd been too weak to go to that concert, so he went by himself, and then his blue eyes weren't focused on me anymore.

When someone told me they'd seen them kissing, I screamed. This was an actual scream,

not pretend, like it came from something outside of myself, and if I didn't let it out, I would
explode. Truly, it felt like I might just die.

Mostly, I was upset I'd never get to feel his
ribcage again.

Starman

My dad's well smart. He can tell you all the planets off by heart and the names of the moons that float around them too. Miss Baker got in a fight with him on parent's evening about it. In lesson, she told us Pluto weren't a planet, and when I told my dad, he said that he'd take it up with her when he saw her next. He didn't forget either. It were the first thing he brought up.

"Heard you're going round telling them Pluto's not a planet."

He said once a planet always a planet, and no one were gonna tell him any different. Miss Baker were all like:

"I'm afraid you're wrong, Mr Nowak. The science has changed…" and Dad went bloody spare. He said that proper science doesn't change. If it changes, it's not really science it's just like, belief, which Dad says is all bullshit anyway. Miss Baker's lips went all thin. She said she disagreed.

I can't tell you what my dad said in response because the words he used I'm not allowed to say. I had to go to loads of meetings after that. They said that I weren't in any trouble, but they wanted to talk. They asked loads of weird questions. I told them my dad was the best dad in the world, and that he could've been an astronaut or a rocket surgeon probably, and Miss Baker just didn't like being wrong. I don't go to that school anymore, though.

Dad says school's rubbish anyway. What they teach you these days you don't even need. It's all writing. Dad hates writing. He says he wants it one way or the other, right or wrong, that's how he likes it. He teaches me everything himself now. He's real good at it. Way more fun than Miss Baker. He were definitely clever enough to be a teacher, my dad, if he'd wanted to be.

Dad doesn't have a job or anything, but that's good because it means he's always about. He got money from the government because his thinking were all different, and he didn't like to conform to everyone else's standards.

"They know a mind like mine is wasted in a supermarket," he used to say, tapping his finger to his head. "Anyway, I've got you to look after, haven't I?"

After a while, we starting getting letters telling him he had to get a job. Dad ignored it first off, told them that they didn't have control of him, and he could do what he liked, but after a while of not paying rent, they put us out.

"Pete, mate, you still have to pay. I've given you enough chances," fat Mr Paulson had said, looking embarrassed while my dad were all red in the face, going mad again. He held up his chubby hands in defence, but I could tell he weren't scared really. Just guilty.

"But what about my boy, ey? What about him?" my dad asked.

That didn't matter though. We ended up going to a place where they gave us a room for free. It were dead small, but that were fine because there were only two of us. Well, not really. There ended up being loads more people. Mostly men with long hair wandering down the corridors. They was always friendly and said hello. Some of them smelled really bad, though. I don't think we smelled very good either. I left with a rucksack with loads of clothes and some of my books and a Gameboy, but that was it. My Gameboy ran out of battery, and then I didn't see the point of having it anymore since I'd forgot to bring the charger. I'd only brought one jumper, and I should've brought more because after wearing it every day, it started to get all musty and gross.

Dad says there's two types of hot. There's hot hot and warm hot. Hot hot, he says, is like when you're on your summer holidays, and you're lying on the beach. He says it's like when you're in the park playing footy, and you have to take your top off and you're sweating. I like that kind of hot but only sometimes. The other type of hot—warm hot—is different. That's like when you're wrapped up in bed and it's raining outside, or when you're all under the blankets on the settee and watching *Star Wars* or something really good like that, with a cup of cocoa keeping your hands warm. I always like warm hot. Sometimes I even like cold weather more because I'd rather be warm hot than hot hot.

Dad tried to get a job. He went to the place to fill out all the forms, and they made him do a test. The computer was slow, and it annoyed him. He clicked on one thing, but it went on another thing, and he accidentally gave the wrong answer. I knew he were getting angry again because he growls when he's annoyed, real quiet and under his breath, but I can still hear it. I knew that he needed to do this because otherwise we wouldn't get our money. I said so. That was when it got really bad. He put his head in his hands and started breathing heavy.

"Dad," I said, trying to calm him down, "it doesn't matter if you fail. You don't have to get the job. You just have to *take* the test and show you're trying. That's how we get the money. If you prove that you're looking by *taking* it." But that didn't help. Dad still lost it. He threw back his chair and shouted, started hitting the computer with the flat palm of his hand. That was scary because the computer were quite thin, and it kept moving as he hit it, and I knew we couldn't afford to pay for it if he broke it. About three staff members came out then and crowded round him.

"Mr. Nowak, I'm afraid you're going to have to leave."

"But the machine, it wouldn't…"

"Mr. Nowak, I'm afraid this time it's your final warning."

So we left. It were pretty sad. I felt scared because I knew that we couldn't stay in that room now, and there probably weren't much chance we could get back to the flat so I could pick up the rest of my stuff, and I still didn't have my Gameboy charger. I shouldn't have been scared, though. Dad always sorts stuff out.

When we go to sleep now, he points up and teaches me all the constellations. That one's the Seven Sisters. This one's Orion's Belt. I know way more about space than probably any other kid my age because I've got my dad teaching me. He still says Pluto's a planet, but it's so far away we can't see it. Once we thought we saw Mars, a big red dot in the sky, but it might have just been an aeroplane. I like being here with Dad because when we share our sleeping bag, I've got his body up against me, and I feel warm hot which is good because most of the time my clothes are wet, and when your clothes get wet, you feel cold right to the bone. It'll be better in summer I reckon, but that's a long way away yet.

Texture

Texture was a tat-shop for hippy bits-and-bobs which sold nothing practical and everything important. Items included, but were not limited to, second-hand non-fiction books, incense sticks and scented candles, Tracy Emin mousemats, Ganesh figurines and keychains, ashtrays hand-glued with gemstones, chunky homemade jewellery with close resemblances to rudimentary musical instruments, and beautiful fabric wall-hangings which draped the shop from floor to ceiling in violet, scarlet, and indigo, making the 10 by 10 space seem like an endless, magical cave. The darkness and the incense smoke made it timeless, and when customers left, stepping back onto the dreary Digbeth streets, they often found themselves blinking in the light.

The owners claimed it was a café; it wasn't really. There was one table in the corner with two chairs and a sofa where you could buy a cup of chai or instant coffee for a quid. The mugs were mismatching, all different sizes and colours, more often than not with cartoon cats or slogans ranging from "A Woman's PLACE is in Her Union!" to "You look Tea-riffic!" This café was almost exclusively used by friends who wanted to chat to the owners for a couple hours and the occasional international student who'd gotten confused by Google maps and wanted a place to read. All were welcome. There was never a time limit for how long you were allowed to stay.

The playlist was mixed and entirely depended on which of the owners shouted the loudest that day. Sometimes it was Joan Jett, Patti Smith, Sinead O'Connor; sometimes it was Bollywood soundtracks with a little UB40; sometimes Bad Manners, often Tracy Chapman, sometimes, but more rarely, a little bit of bhangra. Texture was never busy, but always kept afloat. It was, to one small couple, paradise.

Vex always woke up later than her partner on a Saturday. Her Friday night meetings with the DoBs were sacred, a chance for her to don her leather, play pool, and get tipsy. The next morning was always a bit of a write-off, and Kala would leave Vex snoring between the bedsheets while she pottered off to open.

Kala's quiet in those mornings was a sign of love. She understood how much those nights at the Anchor meant to Vex, and so she didn't tease the hangover, although she might be tempted. If Vex slept in on a Sunday, the hoover would be going by 8 at the latest, but Saturdays were respected, as hobbies in one's autumn years should always be respected.

That's why when Vex's phone rang at 8:10am on a Saturday, she knew she couldn't ignore it and go back to sleep. The confusion with waking up and pushing back the sheets and fumbling with the pillows was too much for her foggy head to cope with, and she missed the call. Initially, she'd thought the tinny ringtone was a dream. Before she could call back, she got Kala's text.

Come to Texture now.

"Fuckkkkk," Vex groaned, hoping to Christ it wasn't another burst pipe. With a full stop like that, it could be nothing good. She pulled on jeans, a fresh vest top to go over her cidery skin, and after one quick deodorant spray, she was off.

It was a miserable day for June, all wet and puddly, and stamping round the Bullring, Vex felt apathy emanating from everyone else who was forced to be up this early on a Saturday. Course, the vote had only been two days ago, and the mood was still a bit glum. Even so, all concrete and drizzle, things felt bleaker than they should.

When she arrived, glass crunched beneath her Doc Martens. Vex had seen the glass but didn't avoid it. Instead, she stepped right on the shards as if to enjoy the crunch, as if to say, "Yeah go on then, you just try and pierce this sole, you piece of shit." It wasn't Vex's first broken window, but it was the first she'd shared with Kala. "PAKIS GO HOME" was graffitied on the outside brick. That was a new one. Vex looked for the trademark NF, but it wasn't there. She supposed it was all Britain First these days. *Anyway, you idiots,* she thought, *Kala's Indian, not Pakistani, and I'm white as alabaster.*

"Lovely!" Vex exclaimed aloud, so Kala would know she'd arrived. Her partner wondered round from the back room, but she didn't say anything. She looked upset, her eyes swollen like she'd just finished crying. Vex suddenly recalled that almost forgotten feeling, the surprise and hurt that followed when you realised this truly was the world you lived in, that people actually were this cruel. That feeling was sprinkled over her adolescence like grit on an icy road, and she ached to take it away from the heart of the woman she loved, to evaporate the feeling entirely and make her feel clean and new again. Well, this might be Kala's first rodeo, but it certainly wasn't Vex's. Back in Shit-Town-Nowhere, where she'd had the misfortune to be born and the idiocy to set up her first business, bricks through windows were a standard. Kala was right to have woken her up. Vex could sort this with swift efficiency.

"Right then. Let's get the brush out and the radio on, shall we?" she said.

Kala nodded. "Tea?" she asked.

"Would murder a coffee, my head's not ideal."

"Good night, was it?" and although it had been, Vex responded:

"Nothing to write home about."

Kala handed over the dustpan and brush. Sweeping was a one-person job, really, so Kala just wrung her hands and looked around, uncharacteristically quiet while the kettle boiled. Vex turned on the radio. BBC 2, golden oldies, why not? There wasn't much point arguing about what to listen to today. None of their favourite songs would fit, after all. What *was* the right musical timbre for a hate crime?

"We'll have to take stock of what we've lost," Kala said eventually.

"Ah babe, don't worry about that. They won't have nicked anything, just smashed up a lot. What do bigots want with old copies of Judith Butler?"

"They slashed my wall-hangings."

"Oh," Vex said. "Okay."

So not just material lost but hours and hours of work. Kala always sat in front of quiz shows on a night, weaving while she shouted things like: "It's Duran Duran, you bloody fools!" at confused and irritating Chase contestants. Vex would have the tea cooking next door, laughing to herself because Kala shouted often at these "bloody fools" on telly, and half the time her answers were dead wrong. Still, it passed the time while she worked methodically with her hands, that great big loom gently pinging in front of her.

"I'm sorry, love," Vex said, watching tears fill Kala's eyes again as she fingered the ripped fabric. Kala never cried, really. She was usually a ray of sunshine, much brighter and friendlier than Vex, far more able to pull in friends. When she was hurt, she was raging. This deflated melancholy was new and unsettling, and Vex scrambled for anything reassuring to say. "We can claim it on insurance, probably."

Not for the first time, Vex cursed her inability to express sympathy properly. It wasn't that she didn't understand; it was just that she couldn't respond right. She was always so practical, practical, practical, never stopping to allow her partner a moment of irrationality even when it could be the difference between a moment of weakness or a bad, bad day. Kala laughed a little but only to hide the sob she felt rising in her throat.

"Well, I suppose if it's covered by insurance, that's alright then."

Unlike Vex, who constantly disparaged her roots in "Shit-Town Nowhere," Kala was very proud of where she'd come from. Her working-class childhood in Ladywood looked grim on the surface, particularly to her grandmother who'd visited England only once before insisting that all family reunions remained in India.

"I like," she'd said with as much calm as her disdain could muster, "my buildings to differentiate from the sky."

Kala had spent her childhood on the Saturday market speaking English and Hindi and (broken) Gujarati. This was where she'd learned to weave, helping her mom for "pocket money" which as a teenager was less than minimum wage. Child bloody labour, she used to call it.

"Child labour," her mom would mutter back. "After all those free meals, the gas, the electric… You should be paying me."

But despite their bickering, Kala loved the market. Even when she was old enough to be nursing a hangover from Nightingales, she enjoyed being close to her mom, eating chips with curry sauce on a lunch time, though *miles* away from the fabric under fear of death.

Kala had always been told her identity should be split, like there were only two sides of her, and both were a dirty little secret she must hide from the other, but she'd never felt that way. Her family was never bothered about the gay thing, as long as she wore a real lehenga for the civil partnership.

"And make it red for your colouring. Yeah, white doesn't suit you," her mother would tut. "Blanches you. Makes you look fat."

When she took her mother for a coffee and told her about Vex, she'd been shaking with nerves. That's when she knew it was real. Everyone else was a simple bit of fun that she hadn't felt the need to mention, but suddenly, right now, it mattered.

"Mom, I'm seeing someone. She's called Vera, and I adore her." She'd said it all in one quick breath, forcing it out like the final push during labour.

"Is she Hindu?" asked her mother, putting down her cup.

"No, Mom. She's white."

"So she's Christian?"

"Definitely not, no. She's not anything, really."

"So, she could be Hindu?"

"Um… maybe. I'm not sure she wants to be."

Her mother tutted irritably. "At least she's not Punjabi."

While Vex cleaned, Kala kept busy too. The mundanely cheerful adverts on the radio made her nauseous and irritated, so she drowned it out by keeping the kettle going for an endless stream of tea. She updated her family chat on WhatsApp and told them of the news. Her father offered her money. A momentous gesture. She declined.

"Vex can sort it on insurance," she tapped.

"Sensible girl," he responded. Her father had approved of Vex ever since she'd changed the spark plug in his old Toyota Corolla. Since her father was an Uber driver, this small act of kindness appealed to two of his favourite personal attributes: frugality and hard-workmanship. He consistently referred to Vex as a "bright young woman, indeed." Vex would snigger to Kala, joking that she shouldn't mention it was a trick she'd learnt from her good ol' friends the Dykes-On-Bikes. Kala doubted he would've minded either way.

"We find out who did it, we'll smash 'em cuz," said the youngest of her nephews, presumably speaking for the three of them.

"Thank you, Karun," she responded with calm.

Her sister and mother gave her an onslaught of kind words and well-intended but irritating questions, and Kala put her phone down. Everyone was lovely. She was so fortunate. Still, it wasn't helping. She was hoping to smother the bad feelings with support, but she couldn't because that fury was still there, insisting that she felt it, and by speaking to her family she was only finding herself directing that fury onto them for reasons that made no sense and would help no one, least of all herself. There was nothing they could say that would make this better. She turned her phone on silent and placed it face down. Almost immediately, it began vibrating, signalling a phone call. She ignored it and switched on the kettle again.

They'd gone to visit Vex's hometown ("Shit-Town Nowhere") only twice, once to visit an ailing father and then later to help move him into a home. Both were miserable trips, the second far worse than the first. Initially, Kala had loved the quaint little high-street, the rolling green fields that spread out like patchwork tablecloths through the passenger window. The house was practically a mansion, and Kala declared that loudly at least three times within five minutes of pulling into the drive. She'd taken Vex's mother's rudeness and her elder sister's spiteful comments as a natural side-effect of the stressful situation, particularly since Vex had spent the entire time practically mute. Clearly no one was feeling especially jolly. Kala's attempts at light-hearted conversation were either brushed off or outright ignored, so eventually she embraced the soberness too, furrowing her brow with the rest of them like she was playing a part in a play.

When the inevitable blow-up happened (and what was it over again? Vex folding her father's clothes incorrectly? Her sister criticising her short haircut? Something so mundane and irrelevant, it was barely worth mentioning), Kala calmly took Vex away from the situation, out for a walk to get some fresh, rousing air. It took about ten minutes for them to find the local pub.

And in their aloneness for those two hours, everything was fine. Fags were lit, complaining flowed. The wholesome, rural accents which whittered in the background felt pleasantly Emmerdale, and the pints were so cheap Kala nearly had a heart attack.

"If we moved here, we could live like queens!" she said, and for the first time since leaving spaghetti junction, Vex cracked a smile. They kissed over their table after a few too many pints, and the bartender decided to cut them off at the next round for their egregious drunken behaviour.

"We have a right," the bee-hived bat proclaimed coldly, "to refuse service to anyone we believe to be over an acceptable limit."

It was so obviously bigoted that Kala couldn't help but laugh. Where she came from there was a whole gay *village*, for god's sake. And had that idiot with her stupid hair not noticed the old man six pints in who couldn't keep his head up, drooling onto his copy of the Daily Mail? (Of *course* it was the Daily Mail). But rather than causing a fuss, Kala left it. Really, she felt she had to. Vex's jaw was so tight that entire weekend that Kala worried she'd chip a tooth.

They never went back to that side of the family, made excuses every holiday, and no one really followed up. Kala stopped making little jibes at Vex's middle-class upbringing. After seeing her home life, it just didn't seem in good taste.

It was the little bits of glass that bothered Vex the most. You can do a big dramatic sweep of the floor, get it all into the bin with a satisfying clash, make the ground neat and beautiful again, but the shelves were full of shit (their premium goods and services) and had to be removed carefully and placed somewhere else until the glass was swept away, and then that same shit (premium goods etc.) had to be placed back bit by bit and still didn't look as good as they did before. It was gentle work, and Vex was impatient and under-stimulated. Glass like grains of sand stung under her nails.

That toad looking bastard was on the radio, sounding as smug as ever. "You all laughed at me. Well, I have to say, you're not laughing now, are you?"

"What an absolute wanker," Vex called out. No response from Kala so she carried on. "I mean, honestly, what's the point of him? Isn't his wife French or something? And his name is Farage!" She donned an over-the-top French accent, placed her fingers in a chef's kiss. "*Fah-rachhhhhe.* Absolute gobshite, that's all I'm saying." Vex laughed a little to herself.

"Are you enjoying this?" Kala asked, her actual fiery personality apparent for the first time that day. "Are you actually happy you get to act all high and mighty, telling off a politician, who is *not* listening to you by the way, after our own community has smashed up everything we've built? Sometimes I swear you get off on acting the liberal."

Vex brushed off the remark, although it stung. The reality was her radicalism was a defence, a crutch she used to navigate the world but, and even she had to admit, that crutch did come in handy as a tool with which to whack people over the head.

"Darl, I know you're sad, but this is just part of it, you know? Honestly, I'm amazed it's not happened sooner."

"Brexit, you mean?"

"No, getting trashed. I mean, come on. We're old lesbians selling modern art and feminist literature. It was bound to happen!"

"Oh, Vex!" Kala sniffed in frustration and sat down on her stool. "This isn't to do with that. It's not to do with you at all."

"You can't blame yourself, love."

"I wasn't, actually," Kala looked up at her, irritated. Like with her family, Vex intended to help, but with this sickness weighing heavy on Kala's soul, every word of reassurance felt off-kilter and unbearable.

"Alright, well look, we're both going through it, so there's no point getting mardy now. There's a ton of brown-owned businesses in Birmingham, and I don't think it's surprising that the racists went after the queers, that's all I'm saying. Hate crimes should be expected."

"Yeah but people don't hate crime *us* for a reason."

"What, you think we're immune?"

"And we *aren't* just old lesbians, and we *don't* just sell modern art and feminist literature. There's also clothes, and traditional art, and candles and things…"

"Is this the stock take you mentioned earlier?"

"And I make cups of tea for all the shops round here. I send Christmas *and* Diwali cards so they know I'm foreign and exotic but not too strange. I talk in the thickest Brummy accent you've ever heard and way too loudly for the pensioners when they pretend not to understand me. I let every 'coloured' and 'queer' slide, I tell white girls they look beautiful in saris, I dress femme, I nod along, I do everything I possibly can to foster a community spirit, and it still means nothing, I… Look."

Kala gestured around the room, although it was now mostly cleared. The slashed wall-hangings swayed in the breeze left by the broken window. Instead of gulping back the lump in her throat, she let the tears run freely down her cheeks.

Vex still didn't know what to say, so she sank to the knees of her denim jeans. She rested her hands on Kala's soft churidar. She'd always found the fabrics Kala wore so nice to touch. It comforted her now, though she was very aware that she wasn't the one who should be comforted.

"We can move if we need to," Vex said. "Go somewhere more open."

"Oh, what's the point? Where would be safer? This is my home. It's not the home they're telling me to go back to, but it is."

Vex held onto her partner's knees and let her head rest on her lap. A moment later, Kala rested her forehead on her partner's crown, and they were silent together in their little, folded knot. Vex felt her hair grow wet and didn't mind. Soon, they'd fight the world. They'd strap on their big, brave Dyke faces and square up but not right now. For now, it was enough to let themselves feel it, the pain, the unaimed rage, the inner guilt, the unjustified shame, the complexity of all of it. There was a time for anger, but for now, they had to touch each other to remind themselves that they were still there, still not alone, both there, apart together.

That Goddamn Cliche Pagliacci

Simon liked the hospital. It was a good place to cry because no one ever stared. It was open 24/7, and everyone spoke softly; interactions were gentle and occasional, instigated only by those with ludicrous levels of self-confidence. When he cried there, people would slip Simon a litt le brochure about Jesus or group-counselling with a look that teetered on the knife-edge between kind and smug.

"Bless you," they'd say, and he'd respond in kind.

Simon had never entered a hospital for any legitimately tragic reason. He'd broken his arm as a child trying to walk on a make-shift tightrope, and once he'd visited a dying grandmother who he couldn't understand and didn't much like anyway, but neither of those occasions he considered to be particularly tragic. When he broke his arm, he got a bright green cast and lots of balloons. The pain, he'd found, was worth the spotlight. The children's ward had been painted with pictures of clowns, and so his fall from the tight-rope, far from discouraging him from the comic arts, instead reinforced all he knew to be brilliant. His grandmother's dying had been depressing, of course, but the fact he'd seen her just at the right moment, death not yet present but imminent, meant that he could walk freely without guilt. Simon associated the hospital with positive things: goodness, pride, attention.

Despite being in for no legitimately tragic reason, Simon ended up crying in the hospital coffee shop near on twice a week. This was a necessary development after he'd been caught crying in a car park, tears smudging down his white, cakey cheeks. The person who tapped on the window to check he was alright couldn't quite hide the smirk behind their faux concern.

"You alright?" they'd asked in a sing-song voice, beanie hat pulled down over faded green hair.

Simon caught sight of himself in the rear-view mirror and was too embarrassed to answer. The smudged red and blue down his white face looked like a barber's pole.

"I would've thought you had a whole troupe back there to cheer you up."

All of it was wrong. This person was too chipper. His car was too yellow. He was in his work gear when he should have been in his own clothes (every clown worth their salt knows work clothes are meant to signify happiness!). Colour in a good mood feels like sunshine. Colour in a bad mood is a headache. With Simon in a bad mood, and the source of all the colour, the nature of his surroundings felt destructive. He started the car and drove off, knowing perfectly well that he would be a joke to this person now, an amusing anecdote, a casebook example of irony in action. This could never happen again.

The hospital was better than any other emergency crying spot, better than crying at home, even. The kind words and sympathetic looks made a difference, and self-conscious as he was to be caught crying in his clown gear, Simon was still an extrovert deep down. Although his social circle was pitifully small, he was concerned someone might recognise him. Thankfully, he had disguises permanently ready in the boot of his car.

His favourite wig looked natural. Natural-looking wigs were difficult to find in the world of clowning; all Simon's other ones were made of a red or orange sponge. His exception was a long, loose, auburn perm that he used for the slightly edgier, sexier performances, the ones with uni-cycles and knife juggling, but those kind of late-night circus performances were rare, much rarer than the kids' parties, so he was glad for another opportunity to wear it while crying in the hos-pital. While the disguise proved so effective that while he wasn't ever recognised as Simon, he *did* begin to be recognised as the ever-present, red-headed crier.

"Excuse me," an elderly woman who approached him started. "I've seen you here before. My Ian just passed, and well… I suppose you've lost someone too?"

There was a gentleness in her eyes, a yearning for understanding that shook Simon's conscience, and he wanted to tell the truth, to say that no, there was no one dying, no one sick, no one at all, in fact, and that was the problem. Sometimes at night when he couldn't sleep, he'd stare into the blackness and beg it to swallow him. He wasn't depressed enough to kill himself, which really would be the sensible thing, because he so desperately wanted to be okay. He stuck flowers on his jacket and squeaked his way to work, full of smiles and grins because if he couldn't put it on (just for a minute, just for the kids) then he knew he'd never be able to smile again. But he couldn't say this to the poor old lady who'd just lost her Ian. Instead, he nodded, letting the tears drip down his cheeks, stinging his sensitive skin, made more sensitive by the regular application of face-paint.

"My wife…" he whispered.

"Oh darling," she said. "Oh darling. And so young!"

Her name was Flo, and they sat and had a coffee together that day. She came in a lot anyway, for her bones, she said, and so they ran into each other often. Sometimes she even brought in her daughter who was still (this said with a wink) single, if he was interested. But no, his heart would only ever belong to Josephine (his imaginary dead wife's name. He thought of the dancer with bananas on her skirts, swirling around with those perfect hip motions).

To stop others from catching on, wondering why he kept hanging around this hospital like one of the many bad smells, he conjured up a child, a small baby hooked up in an incubator, forever loved despite being the cause of his mother's untimely death. Simon worried if this might be too Victorian, but no one questioned him. He supposed childbirth was timeless in its brutality.

Flo was wonderful at community building. She texted Simon (although she regularly forgot his name, only ever referring to him as "you poor boy," which hardly mattered because he'd told her his name was Michael) whenever she was going to be at the hospital, and he'd stop by to say hello, and together they would cry. Others joined too, mostly geriatric, finding safety in conformity. Suddenly, a corner of the café was reserved for them, and many sat around with little paper cups, crying together, then talking together, and before anyone knew it and against all likelihood, laughing together too. Simon's story tended to give people a much-needed sense of perspective. With Josephine gone, and now little Kenny likely to go too (though still fighting on, the brave soldier), a dead husband or two didn't seem quite so tragic.

It was in these meetings he met Ernestine.

Now, as Ernestine herself often said, she didn't really belong in the group. She'd never lost anyone through the unforgiving process of death. She *had*, however, lost the use of her legs in a work accident involving a fall from a ladder and a broken back, and with the use of her legs, she'd also lost a boyfriend, who *had* quite fancied her before she'd ended up becoming quite so "needy." Ernestine now openly wept, apologising the entire time, because who was she to cry? She still had *her* son, and he was in good health, and when she thought about what poor Michael was going through…

"It's okay." Simon would nod solemnly.

… she really knew she had absolutely no right to complain.

"Loss is loss." Simon smiled at her. "There's no need to compare."

Ernestine hated her ex, partner of four years, father to their three-year-old, who still hadn't proposed evidently because he'd had no intention of committing. She spoke of the loss of him bitterly, more angry at this than the loss of her legs, because at least her legs would work if they were *able* to. Si (her ex-boyfriend, an awful coincidence) had just fucked off. Didn't even try. And they *could* have gotten through it together…

"It's selfish," Simon agreed.

… and he'd said he loved her.

"Dishonest."

Clearly it hadn't meant a thing. She should have listened to her mother.

When Ernestine had finished her little speech, she looked at Simon with a small, sweet smile. Ernestine later told him she'd never felt able to complain so openly. She'd been raised to understand that everything was in God's plan for her, every black cloud, every moment of suffering. She didn't believe in bad luck, just a bad attitude, and she'd raised her boy Daniel accordingly. She wanted him to be a happy child. That was looking increasingly less likely. Half the time he had to spend his days with *her* mother (his grandmother), who'd been quick with the switch and a harsh word back in the day, something Ernestine wanted to avoid being a believer in gentle parenting after her strict upbringing caused her to be so terribly insecure. But how could she care for him during her weeks in the hospital? And his dad was no use. Whenever she caught Daniel's eye these days, he looked sad. And wise. That was what scared her the most. His eyes held that dark-brown soulful quality that demonstrated suffering, and the boy was three years old.

Simon didn't quite know what to say to this. It saddened him too. Children's eyes should be opened wide in fascination, never sad. Wisdom was something they should get far, far, later in life. This was why he indulged in the silly, still hoping to capture that spark of youthful wonder.

He hadn't meant to do it so brazenly, but gosh she'd touched a nerve. Simon leant forward to hold her hand.

He memorised Ernestine's physiotherapy time-table. He stopped coming in just to cry. The coffee was too sweet as he waited for her (in his anxiety, he tore up all the sugar packets) but still he drank it though it coated his teeth in an uncomfortable, sickly fashion. When she wheeled into the café, he waved at her.

"I didn't know you'd be here today." She smiled.

Simon shrugged.

"Got to make the time for our Kenny."

And Ernestine tilted her head in sympathy and took his hand in hers.

Hand-holding became something of a treat for them. When she left him, his palm tingled for the rest of the day, and during the act, he felt peace. They didn't even have to speak. They sighed. They smiled. At times, she was so tired after physio that he'd help lift her out of her chair, and they'd move onto the booth with the comfy sofa cushions, their hands still entwined, and he'd watch her. Then came the blessed day where she lolled her head onto his shoulder and slept. She smelt like coconuts. When she woke, she apologised.

"Oh God, Mike, I'm sorry! How awkward. I hope that wasn't uncomfortable for you."

"Not at all." He shook his head. "Your hair smells like coconuts."

"Is that a good thing?"

"Very."

"Well, that's good. I like your hair too."

She leaned forward to touch a strand of it. He let her, unconcerned about wig-slippage because Simon was an expert in bobby-pinning.

"You know," she said, "my first crush was another Michael. Mick Hucknall. From Simply Red. Do you know him?"

Simon nodded, conscious that her hand was still touching a strand of his hair, that their faces were close together now, that as she'd turned her head to look up at him, her body was now facing his, and it would only take the slightest movement from him to indicate he wanted to kiss her. He must have made it. She leant in. And Simon blessed the hospital, blessed his natural-looking wig, blessed Mick Hucknall, blessed the world, blessed Si even, the bastard ex, because now things were coming together, and he didn't have to feel so alone.

There is no crime more despicable than infanticide. Simon had known this intrinsically for years. It went against his very nature to hurt a child. His work was supposed to be a celebration of childlike joy, but now he knew he had no choice. Little Kenny couldn't recover. As much as he wished for it, it would be an impossibility. The moral dilemma had kept him awake at night as he thought about himself and Ernestine and Daniel and little baby Kenny pulling together to make a beautiful family, but the adoption process seemed like far too much hard work, and unless he risked coming clean (ridiculous at this stage), he knew that Kenny had to die.

There wasn't a funeral. It would have been too sad. He gave the body to science so they could have a look at the organs, or whatever it was that scientists did, and hopefully that would help future children avoid such an awful fate. It seemed like the kindest thing to do. Ernestine held him while he cried on their favourite booth, rocking him while he sobbed like he was a child himself until his head fell on her lap, and she stroked his (firmly enforced) hair.

The tears were real. Killing a baby is not an easy thing to do. The time had come, though. Simon could not stay crying in the hospital café anymore; something needed to shift.

Not Simon now, Michael. It's Michael to me and to everyone who matters. Simon is my work name. Well, my work name is Captain Sprinkles, but to the other clowns, it's Simon, but really I'm Michael, no really I am, not a clown, no, Michael, a singer, a rockstar Mick, ol' Micky boy, don't you forget about me, Mick. Wait, is that Simply Red? No, I think that's Simple Minds.

Easily done. Always mix those up. Typical Simon, no Michael, it's Michael it's…

Michael had never met anyone so strong before. Ernestine held her head high in every situation, unflinchingly bold, heartbreakingly powerful.

They had gone to the cinema on their first official date. The cinema was a wonderful opportunity to hide in the dark and hold hands. The film was a comedy, but Michael hadn't laughed at all, not because it wasn't funny, just because he felt better smiling to himself, his head atop Ernestine's as they breathed in that lovely popcorn smell. It was raining, but inside they were warm and dry, just the two of them on their own row where the wheelchair space was reserved.

They kissed at the bus-stop. The bus was ten minutes late, but neither of them cared. Like teenagers, they giggled, noses rubbing together, and Michael only just stood up in time to signal the bus to stop. The bus driver opened the door, shaking his head.

"No room for the chair, mate. Too many buggies."

Michael wondered why he was speaking to him and not Ernestine.

"When's the next one?" she asked.

"Should be along in half an hour."

"Can no one fold their buggy up?" she asked, disheartened.

Another shake and the bus drove off.

Michael was delighted at the news. Unaffected by this clear display of ableism, he thought only of the extra thirty minutes he had to kiss her in the rain, but when the bus had driven off, and he went to lean in again, she suddenly seemed cold and stiff, her eyes trained forward not seeing him, not really seeing anything. To kiss her felt grotesque. Instead, he held her hand. The next bus was ten minutes early and ready with the ramp, but Michael knew it wasn't really about the wait. Ernestine didn't recover her energy that night. Their adolescent-like excitement had evaporated, and Michael settled for a demure kiss on the cheek by her front door. She responded with a wan smile and a promise that she'd call soon.

The next day he modified his Beetle with hoists. He'd drive them on dates from now on. He couldn't change the world, but he could do his best to make their own world safe. This change involved a removal of the car boot's disguises. He moved them to the bottom of his wardrobe, the wigs hidden in plastic bags beneath the shoes, thinking his life as a clown must be organically, happily, coming to an end.

Despite this new beginning, Simon still had to work. The world of children's entertainment was not lucrative, and he couldn't pass up any opportunity that came a-knocking.

These days, it was only at work-events that Simon deigned to take off his sexy, loose, Mick Hucknall perm. Even without Ernestine, he slept in it. It was a comfort blanket in a way, a reminder that the Simon he knew was now in the past, and he could begin, as Michael, to move on. But until he found a new job (preferably in insurance, which is where he'd told Ernestine he worked; a mistake on his part as he was terrible on the phone), he was forced to continue clowning.

He removed his tangled Hucknall wig and placed it carefully on its mannequin heads.

"I've missed this beautiful hair," said the mannequin. "The other wigs are so unflattering that if I had eyes, I would surely weep."

"Don't forget this is temporary," Michael warned. "I'll be back to wearing it soon."

"Alas," the mannequin head pined, and Simon set off for work.

This birthday party was a sad one, he'd been told by the agency. The child was turning four and a child of separation. The mother had been firm on the phone, wanting only the best for her son, strict in her conviction that the best clown be sent.

"But he was busy, so we've asked you instead," said the agent who Simon found tiresome.

He came prepared with balloons, a unicycle, juggling bats, balls, and knives, for Simon knew that if the kids seemed unimpressed, a sense of danger usually perked them up. And unimpressed the child did seem, holding his grandmother's hand, his eyes appearing strangely earnest and subdued. The afternoon was bright. The rain had stopped, the clouds had cleared, and what a lucky boy he was, his grandmother had told him in her firm Caribbean accent, to have the sun come out to wish him happy birthday.

Simon juggled the bats, legs kicking side-to-side. The boy still didn't crack a smile, although his nursery pals seemed to adore it, laughing with wide mouths showing off their tiny, square teeth.

"Now, say thank you to Mr. Captain Sprinkles," said his grandmother as the first skit ended.

"Thank you, Mr. Captain Sprinkles," the boy said, keeping eye-contact and a firm voice, seeming far too old for four. Simon knew this would require extra zhuzh.

He changed the music. Out came the unicycle and the knives. A recorded voice played over the Alice Cooper's "Poison," a bass-deep, gravelly, American voice:

"Ladies and gentleman, we require you to stand back. These next stunts can be dangerous. Do not try this at home. We repeat: do NOT try this at home."

The nursery pals all shuffled back dramatically on their bottoms, and Simon could see it was working. Daniel's eyes were wide as coins as he mounted the unicycle.

Build-up was the key. First came the juggling of the batons (frankly unimpressive except for the added thrill of the unicycle), then the batons and the balls together while he stood up from the seat (more impressive, but still the only risk was a short fall), then Simon reached for the knives… No. Not yet. He shook his finger at the children as though to warn them of the danger, and they laughed. Then, with a little fluid from his pocket, a quick spark from his lighter, and BAM! The batons were on fire. The juggling continued.

The children shrieked and whoooooaaed in unison, and Daniel's mouth fell open as he clasped his grandmother's hand. Even she let out a small: "Lord, Jesus."

Which Simon took to mean she was impressed.

The next time he reached for the knives, he grabbed them. Juggling balls, batons on fire, and now three knives added into the mix. Simon watched them twirling in the sky, soaring. He maintained an intense concentration, knowing if he lost it, there would be disaster, but when had Simon ever lost concentration before? He was a professional. He was a maverick. Simon was born to clown.

Ernestine rolled onto the deck into, what Simon now realised, was her mother's back garden, smiling at the sight of her son finally acting his age. Her eyes looked like a cool glass of water, a warm jacket, a service station toilet, looked, in short, like relief. And while she sighed at her son, her shoulders dropping back, Michael was quite conscious that if she looked at the performer then she'd see that it was him, a slightly startling career change for her boyfriend who was supposed to be in insurance, and he'd have to think how to explain this, *while not breaking concentration, eyes always on the knives, feet always on the pedals, Simon!*

No, not Simon. Michael. No. Not Michael. Captain Sprinkles. No. One look could kill, my pain, your thrill. No. You make-a me feel brand new. No. Don't you forget about me? No! Simple Minds, god damn it, Simply Red, not Simple Minds. Mick Hucknall, no Simon, no Captain Sprinkles. No Michael, no...

'Mr. Captain Sprinkles, no!' shouted Daniel right before the accident.

Tone Deaf

Giles no longer found white women attractive. Their shoulders were too wide, their voices too loud, and their ideologies detestable. English white women in particular expected a subservience that Giles absolutely refused to kowtow to, and rightly so, as the obedience they craved still seemed to leave them unsatisfied. No. They were spoiled, ungrateful, and entitled, with completely inflated senses of self-importance which repelled him entirely, repelling him across oceans and continents, no less.

He hadn't always felt this way. In his first marriage, Giles was vaguely happy with his wife. She was conservative and loyal with a sense of common decency. That affection had faded as the years went on, and after gaining twenty pounds and losing all her sex appeal, she'd left. Two years later, after a string of awful courting attempts,

Giles left too. He hadn't stepped foot on British soil in over 15 years.

The women in Chengdu were much more manageable. They were sweeter, with quiet, soft-spoken voices. Their frames were slight and girlish in a way that Giles had always found appealing.

Moving had been a snap decision, so "snap" that many of his acquaintances equated it to a mid-life crisis.

"To China? You're kidding! Well, I suppose he likes travelling. And after the divorce, and all. It does seem strange, going all that way. And the language barrier!"

But the East had always held an exotic appeal for him. It started on his honeymoon, travelling with Taiwan Airlines, seeing the dainty, young women in their blue uniforms and red lipstick. He liked the way they served him whisky and insisted on calling him "sir" in their darling, incorrect accents. The happy couple were on their way to Bangkok via Taipei. Giles found the flight-attendants so utterly charming, although his wife was completely oblivious, her own round eyes drilling the in-flight magazine for duty-free perfumes. Giles worried then that getting married young may have been a mistake.

After the initial TEFL training, in which Giles was thrust into a sweaty room with awful people in their early twenties, Giles created the framework for his new life. The teaching was somewhat enjoyable, and the children behaved appropriately. In a few years, he'd managed to build his own English school, hiring a number of wonderful Western and Chinese staff alike. His apartment was extensive—white walls and carpeted floors with huge glass windows overlooking the winter smog. Winter was his favourite part of the year. He never had to worry about sweating through his shirts. Most importantly, in winter there were food-stalls outside his apartment block, selling unbearably spicy kebab sticks to warm up his stomach during the freezing nights. Over the years, Giles had grown fond of the stall, particularly of the young girl who worked there. Her name, he'd established, was Newar.

In China, one could easily categorise girls by their ages. There were chubby children, shy teens, ambitious twenty- and thirty-year-olds, and finally, elderly women, heavily lined in the forehead and jowls, stoic, strong, and utterly sexless. The food stall was a family business. The mother's pride visibly grew as she stooped farther forward each year, watching her daughter serve customers with an increasing amount of competence. It was a wonder Newar didn't have a beau, Giles often thought, being as charming as she was. Then again, the girl was likely hesitant to leave her family unit—something very common in these parts, community society and all that—at least not until there was a rich husband to save her. Giles thought he may be able to offer such a chance at liberation.

She wasn't exactly the most beautiful woman he'd ever seen, but she was pretty. There was an honesty to her stubby nose and crooked teeth. Giles remembered with embarrassment the first time he'd properly spoken to her. He'd grabbed the spices from her hand before she could tip them onto his food and gestured with an emphatic shake of his arms.

"No!"

"Bu yao la ma," she had responded, something he supposed indicated a lack of comprehension because her eyes were wide and shocked. He pointed again to the spice, shook his head slowly and deliberately, making it as easy as possible for her to follow.

"No!"

She nodded, her lips pressed tightly together, and turned around his plain kebab sticks on the grill. This never would have worked with her mother, who often batted him away when he tried to insist on what he wanted. Of course, with the mother, he never would have grabbed the spice from her hand outright. Although she was small and decrepit, Giles imagined she might be able to cause some damage.

The next time he went to the stall, the daughter rushed over as her mother went to pick up the spices. They chattered away like musical clocks until the mother reluctantly put the spices down and followed his instructions. He could only presume he'd caused offence, considering her face as she handed him the box of plain meat. The daughter turned to Giles and smiled, thumbs-up and grinning like a child. For some reason, despite never having thought much of her before, Giles' heart swelled. They were on a team, it seemed, being a little mischievous.

That night she visited him in his apartment. How she had known it was his, he couldn't be sure, but he imagined that she'd been thinking about him for some time and was keen to see where all that money and sophistication hung its hat. To his surprise, she spoke fluent English, although her accent was somewhat tainted by her upbringing. He opened a bottle of wine for them to share.

"And does your mother know where you are?" he asked her. She looked at him and shrugged.

"I could be in worse places."

Later, they made love on the leather sofa under silver lamp-light. Giles was in awe at the way her breasts, so small and delicate, held themselves up entirely, soft and firm to the touch. Her waist dipped inwards, the perfect placement for his hands as he moved her up and down, feeling her warmth. She was enthusiastic, moaned gorgeously, often seeming shocked by the sensations, as though she hadn't believed such pleasure were possible.

It became a regular arrangement. If he didn't visit the stall, she wouldn't come. If he did, she would smile at him, and later they would have their fun. At night, he lay awake with visions of her panting face as she bounced on top of him, and

Giles felt a comfort almost akin to love. He looked over at the stall from the height of his apartment and analysed her crooked teeth, her stubby nose, her sleek black hair, and pockmarked skin. She was so very beautiful.

Giles' interest in his staff disintegrated, and he found himself indifferent to the way his secretary would lean over his desk to point out issues in the school calendar, something he usually admired. This accidental monogamy became something like love. Yes, it was almost like love.

In his apartment she would speak to him:

"I don't like to use English so much in front of my mother. It unsettles her."

"It does?"

"Of course! Not everyone appreciates the beauty of such a language. Mandarin is all the same sounds, repeating and clanking like machinery. English represents itself so proudly. I think that many are afraid of that."

"Yes," Giles answered, "I wholeheartedly agree." He had never deigned to learn Mandarin, finding the whole thing impossible. He initially thought that if he persisted living here for long enough, it would soak into his mind through osmosis, but in the end, there was no need. There were enough translators in his company, and as the boss, he could live as he pleased.

His darling girl, Newar, shared his sentiment. Indeed, he often taught her new words, read her English poems as they lay together under thick blankets. She would point to the sentences that she hadn't fully understood, and he'd explain them to her in a gentle and meticulous manner while she looked at him with the same wide-eyed, uncomprehending expression he'd grown to adore. Teaching English was never his passion more than in these moments.

Soon, Giles ate kebab sticks every day, staring from the window, waiting for the stall to close so that his little sweetheart could scuttle up the stairs and knock on his apartment door. Giles was spending more and more of his time brooding by the glass window. He knew that English women could never make him feel this level of excitement, could never inspire in him such curiosity; for white women who knew poetry presumed they knew it all, and those who didn't care for it were vapid and yet equally as arrogant.

One day, staring out of the apartment window, he watched her at the stall. She was talking to another customer, some Asian man with a black fleece jacket and bad teeth. He was younger than Giles. Younger but uglier too. Newar laughed at his jokes, touched his arm, and this would have all been acceptable were it not for the mother. The mother detested the thought of flirtation. Giles could tell by the way she'd been intervening between them as of late. She got in between the two youngsters and reallocated her daughter to another task. It occurred to Giles then that this young man was not a customer. He too was grabbing baskets, pouring spices onto barbecue sticks. A brother, perhaps? But no, the way they always caught each-other's eyes was apparent. Eight storeys up and Giles could sense their shared affection.

Incensed, he grabbed his jacket to storm across the road and demand an explanation from her. Her secret lessons would no longer be kept secret. He would reveal their activities, shame her appropriately!

The elevator had never before seemed quite so creaking and untrustworthy. The journey down seemed longer than usual. Across the road, he could see her, but as he stormed over for confrontation, his impatience led him straight into a line of traffic where a motor scooter knocked him down. When he hit his head on the concrete, he saw orange fireworks. The scooter drove on unashamedly amidst the shouts. The stall owners rushed across the road, the mother first as she crouched down to speak to him, the same incoherent Chinese warbling.

"Your daughter," he tried to say. "I need your daughter."

"Ting bu dong," the mother said, one of the only expressions he'd learned in Chinese, and one that always brought him intense frustration.

The daughter took over from her mother's place.

"Hello," she said in a stronger accent than he'd remembered. "You want hospital?"

"Oh stop that," he'd said, moaning as he sat up. "I know your English is fluent. You can speak better than that."

"Ta ting bu dong," she said again to her mother. Why did her voice sound so different now? The accent was strange. In his apartment, had she been more Taiwanese-sounding? He caught a glimpse of her breasts under her jumper. They were larger today.

"You speak English!" he accused her.

"A little," she admitted. "You want hospital?"

It wasn't the same girl. That he was sure of. She had the same face, stood in the same place by the stall, wore the same apron, but this girl knew nothing of poetry.

"I should confront you," he said, waving a finger at her. His head was hot where he'd hit it, and blood was dripping down. Where was he exactly? What was happening? A crowd was starting to gather round. This was the last thing Giles had wanted.

"I know you speak English," he implored. The girl looked at him with the same wide eyes he remembered, but this time, he could sense she felt *he* was stupid. There was an awkward smirk across her face, revealing second-hand embarrassment.

"English," she said. "Yes. A little." She called over to the Asian youth with the bad teeth, who'd stayed behind to watch the stall. They chattered together in Chinese for a while before turning back to Giles.

"Do you need help?" he said, and his accent was slightly more natural, which Giles resented. It could not be the same girl.

He stood up on shaking legs. Slowly, he turned back to his apartment, feeling his age for the first time. He heard the girl say to her mother behind her. "Ta ting bu dong," but Giles knew how wrong they were. He understood. He understood perfectly.

Mother, daughter, boyfriend shrugged together, stuck between confusion and indifference. Eventually, the mother ushered them back over to the stall. The fire was still going and their meat was burning. The customers were waiting.

Meng Mei (which was, indeed, her real name, only referred to as nü'er by a sweet, indulgent mother) felt relieved to see him storm away. That laowai had been turning up every night at her stall, and while she didn't mind grilling meat with the spices off, she'd started to dislike the leers. That's why she brought her friend along; she knew that he could serve him for a change, save her that creeping sense of inexplicable violation. She was doubly pleased she brought him now, as it seemed the laowai had finally lost his mind.

Anyway, there was nothing more they could have done to help the man. Why try to help someone who didn't want the help? Why try to help someone who just wouldn't understand?

Trinity

George had left the workshop until last because he knew it would be miserable, but it was even worse than he'd expected. Something must have died amongst the wildlife and detritus because the thick smell of decay invaded his nose and mouth. In good weather, his father's greenhouse/workshop brought in light, but now the grey sky closed oppressively around him, and the grass lay soggy and wilting outside. Rain hammered against the walls and sloped off the roof in waterfalls.

No doubt the rain was intolerable, but George preferred it to the stifling heat from the funeral where he sweated through his suit and felt disgustingly alive. There was something grotesque about the burial. George considered the proximity of his father's body slowly lowering down next to his long-deceased wife, rotting away in their forever homes. George imagined the bones of his mother and the bloated stomach of his father as he disintegrated beside her and was impatient to throw the ashes to ashes, dust to dust, so that they could end this morbid pageantry. It had been a quiet affair. His father was, at best, a loveable eccentric, at worst, a social pariah.

Since hearing about his father's cardiac arrest, George had tried practising the word, shaping it around his mouth like bubble-gum. "Orphan." There was something Victorian about it, something archaic that didn't sit right. What would be a better, more suitable term, he wondered. A parentally challenged child? But George hadn't been a child for a long time. He'd hoped that the birth of his own son would allow him to slip into an understanding of family and become a more complete person, but if anything, it had made him feel even more estranged from the rest of the world. For years he'd fantasised about being the supportive and loving role-model he'd never had, the antithesis to his own father, but that was never going to be the case. He was stiff, awkward, overly formal when faced with his son, convinced that he was being mocked in ways he couldn't follow. His wife too seemed in on the joke. When he heard them chattering away together (usually indecipherable nonsense), he felt a sting of rejection despite knowing they intended to include him.

George hadn't expected to be left anything in the will. He hadn't spoken to his father in years, which George had intended to be a punishment although he had his suspicions that his father hadn't noticed. But as it turned out, he'd been wrong. His father must have still thought about his son because he left him everything he owned.

His childhood home was now awfully dilapidated and would never make a profit unless George put some real effort into restoring it, but he had no intention of doing that. He gave himself a week. He'd clear out everything in a yard-sale and drive the rest to the tip. He wouldn't decorate, but he'd clean. There would be no scent of freshly baked cookies but instead one of bleach and polish. Empty. Sterile. He'd accept the first offer, regardless of its stinginess.

The plants in his father's workshop were dying from lack of water, yet still they'd expanded to an almost jungle-like quantity, towering over the books piled atop shelves that were intended, almost certainly, for plant pots. Crucifixes dangled from the glass ceiling. Formaldehyde jars displayed things George refused to examine. If he couldn't sell them to some macabre taxidermist in the yard-sale, they too would go straight in the skip. He clung onto his bin bag in preparation.

In the corner, hidden beneath it all, was the old writing desk. All George's childhood memories of his father consisted of his back hunched over this desk as he scribbled aggressively, neurotically, muttering to himself as he did so. Sometimes George would come in to say hello, and his father would ignore him. He'd see the flicker in his eye that indicated he'd been seen and heard, but no words were spoken. The pain of being ignored felt physical and contributed, no doubt, to the chronic stomach-ache that had defined his childhood. George had always been a sickly boy. He thought that he'd recovered from it all until the sight of the rickety garden furniture, the statues of Hindu goddesses with swinging arms and elephant heads, the hieroglyphs and psychedelic artwork, brought up a vile taste of bitterness and a sickness in his guts.

He swept everything into the bin bag. These things would be worth a fair amount of money, he was sure, but he didn't want to pore over anything from this desk. The theological volumes thumped as they hit the floor, and the sacredness of the materials alongside their desecration felt pleasingly ironic.

He wished his father had been a Frankenstein. A mad scientist was at least something a child could understand. He could have endured some Einsteinian character with a shock of fluffy hair, a lab coat and a chemical vial. If his insanity had been backed up by genius, it might have been worth it.

George found the piles of notebooks and barely flicked through the pages. It was nonsense scribbling, his father's handwriting deteriorating as madness and arthritis got the best of him. The moleskins were stained in different colours. Red, green, blue, lilac. He opened the side drawer and found the last one, small, black, and leather, a post-it stuck onto the front, a biro scratch spelling out: *The Answer.*

George's father never owned a computer. Algorithms terrified him. He didn't trust what they might do with his information (*What information?* George always wondered). Anyone normal would have typed up a manuscript and backed it up online but not George's father. Like a small boy at school, he'd copied out the words time and time again until they were as neat as possible, every letter placed with perfect spacing. George read:

Prologue:

> *My darling Georgiana and I loved fiercely. Although we disagreed on almost everything insignificant, our values were identical, and my girl made sure I stood by them steadfastly even when temptation crossed my heart or anger would distort my thinking. She always managed to make the stars shine brighter, right up until the day she passed away.*
>
> *It was different then. Terminations weren't considered an everyday procedure, and doctors would always attempt to convince potential mothers to fully consider the operation before committing. The permanence of such a decision was very much stressed. Except, that is, in our case. We were told very early into the pregnancy that something was wrong. This was*

easy to believe. Georgiana was in agony and could barely stand. An ambulance had to be sent for, and after the first scan, the doctor was adamant. Her child would kill her and likely die itself in the process.

I begged, pleaded for her to reconsider, but my Georgiana had her mind made up. She could never and would never actively harm one of God's creatures. Not once did I see her resolve quiver. She said she had no fear of heaven. Why would she? I had told her enough times she was an angel, and now she was ready to return home.

Our son survived, although premature and struggling with chronic sickness from infancy to adolescence. The same could not be said for our dear Georgiana. She held him to her chest as she passed away, blood haemorrhaging from her, and she promised me that this was what she wanted, and that one day we'd all be reunited.

I dare say the loss of her would've been enough to spark a demise into insanity, but intellectual necessity brought me out of it. I needed to know if she was right in her assumptions. Naturally, I considered Paley's Watch and the usual dips into theism that many grieving people find a comfort in, but I went further, reading the mythology, the history,

and all the cynicism caught up in between.
This book is not an argument, nor is it a theory
to be considered. Within these pages, you will
find nothing but indisputable fact. There is
an answer. Challenge it if you must, but it
will be of no use. I pray you use this informa-
tion wisely.

George considered reading the whole thing from cover to cover right there and then. A thin volume, it wouldn't take very long. He didn't want to, though. His stubbornness was emotionless but all the same consisted of resolve. He delayed putting the house on the market. First, he felt compelled to contact a publisher.

George typed it up one word at the time, so focussed on the task that he didn't take in any of the content. He kept it loyal to his father's word with only surface-level edits, although he deleted any mention of himself as those sentences seemed to cause a strange stabbing sensation in his abdomen.

The book sold well. Well enough to refurbish the house. Well enough to make a nice little nest-egg for himself. Well enough that George felt it would be a shame to abandon his father's memory altogether.

His wife and son moved into his old home with little stress. On the first night there, they had a bonfire, sacrificing all the dead plants and rat-bitten furniture. The smoke stung their eyes, but George didn't blink. The old copies of the moleskins were used as fuel. They burned well. His wife and child went inside as the sky grew darker, night spreading like an oil spill. George stayed out with a tumbler of whisky. For the first time in a while, he felt able to toast his father's life and poured his libations onto the flames, jumping back as they rushed out to greet him. He laughed, imagining this to be his father's spirit's last hurrah.

In an upstairs bedroom, the curtains twitched. His son looked down at George with something that might have been fear or perhaps just confusion. George raised the glass to him, waving slightly, grinning in his euphoric and slightly drunken state. The child's expression remained the same. The curtains closed.

Trypanophobia: A Triptych

Egypt

Your eyes rolled back into your head, and for a while, everyone could just see the whites. You don't remember this. You remember sickness. You remember fear. Try not to. It's best if you don't remember this.

You were suffering from dehydration. You wouldn't drink water or take your medication. You wouldn't eat.

The doctor came into the hotel room, and you hadn't known he was coming. Your family hadn't told you for a reason. Your arms were too thin for the injection. You cried. Your sister laughed. They had to hold you down because you wouldn't stop squirming. Your family was embarrassed. When the needle entered you, you screamed. You swore you'd never forgive them. It's best if you don't remember this.

You were told the sickness was your fault. They were right. You could've eaten, but you didn't. Everyone was angry at you. You ruined a nice holiday by being so stubborn. You went back to eating normally as soon as you landed, and no one understood why. For a while, everyone hated you. Try not to think about this.

In the holiday photos, you look like a corpse, so you make sure to throw them away. You don't want them to know they were right. It's best if you don't remember this.

England

She asks you to inject her. She says it's fine, she's let other people do it, and now she wants you to. Just in her stomach, right *here*. She deliberately gained weight because she knew she had to get all these injections when her legs were reset. She calls her stomach her little shelf. It's cute that way. It makes her not worry so much about getting fat. Yes, she knows she isn't fat but still.

You don't *have* to do it, but it helps her with the pain. It's worse when she has to do it herself. Actually, she's gotten used to it now. It was hard at the hospital when the nurses were watching over her to make sure she did it properly, and her fingers would slip. Then again, it's not like she should care about a teeny tiny needle after all this surgery. But it's funny, isn't it? Because she does still care. Even when her life is disintegrating and she has to learn how to walk again, she still worries about little things like needles. If you can just hold it, just hold it there. You just have to jab it in and push down on the plunger. She's calm. It won't hurt her. She needs her medication.

You still can't do it. You hand her back the needle and watch her do it to herself.

Sorry, you tell her. It's just too weird.

She asks you if you're scared of needles. You watch her pull it out of her skin without flinching. You're not scared of needles, no, you tell her. You don't tell her that you're terrified of screams.

China

They need to make sure you aren't HIV positive. If you are, they'll deport you. It was part of the medical test, and you wonder if that's homophobic or if you're being too sensitive again. You watch the needle going into your forearm now. You are no longer squeamish. You've done this a million times.

First it was hepatitis,

Then rabies,

Japanese Encephalitis…

All those travel necessities. You want the nurse to think you're brave even though you're an adult and you don't speak the same language. You stare at the needle as you watch it go in. The skin puckers up slightly around the point like a splinter. It's yanked out efficiently when she's done. You smile, stand up with a cotton ball taped to your arm, thank her with incorrect pronunciation.

The hysterical girl is in the blood-booth at the end. She won't stop shaking. Her cries make you flinch. Another white teacher explains it to you. Phobia, they say. She got a doctor's note telling them that she'd already been checked in England and not to do a repeat. The Chinese doctors won't accept it.

At this point, she starts screaming.

You want to tell the screaming girl it doesn't hurt, but you don't because that's not the point. You want to tell her that it's over in a few seconds, but you don't do that either because, again, that's not what matters. You want to smile at her as though you understand, but know she won't think you understand at all.

It's time to move onto the ultrasound ward. They need to examine your empty womb. In the hallway, you hear her scream again. Your body inexplicably starts aching. It's best if you don't remember this.

White Rainbow 2028

It snowed at Pride that year. The crisp, white flakes landed on shoulders like chronic dandruff, and the queers twirled round in their dresses to welcome it. They'd all known it was too cold for June, but the occasion called for strappy, rainbow dresses and high heeled boots, and leather vests, and fishnet stockings and all the sexy, swishy fabric one was wont to wear to scream out love.

Of course, it wasn't magic. Already, they'd lost cities to the ocean. Already, there were famines, empty shelves in supermarkets where the fruit was bruised and bitter, but hey it kept them skinny! (a problematic consolation, but a consolation none-the-less).

And everyone who danced was clever enough to know that this was Not Good. There shouldn't be long Indian summers well into November. We shouldn't be building bridges to the houses lost at sea. It shouldn't really snow at Pride, but fuck it. It was their day. And when they'd glued themselves to roads, they'd been arrested, so instead the road became their glittering stage. And when they'd desecrated art, they'd been condemned, so now they were content to be the art themselves.

With neon wigs and orange skin and flags and floats and Kylie Minogue, with short-shorts and Elvis quiffs and motorcycles and glitter bombs and love and love and love and love and love.

And yes, it shouldn't snow at Pride, but my darling, if our ancestors taught us anything, it's the art of dancing through disaster.

Book Club Questions

1) What does "Cooked Blue" say about the state of the world? Do you agree with the outlook? What details struck you and why?

2) What does "Declutter" illustrate about relationships? Why do you think Brian climbs inside the wardrobe at the end?

3) How does "Depressive Giant Nightmare Boy" address the concept of the manic pixie dream girl? How does making this a first-kiss story affect that dynamic?

4) What do you make of Toni in "Dirty Stop-Outs"? Do you think she'll be back? Is the narrator a good friend to her or not?

5) How do you feel about Lavinia and the distance between what "we" want for her and what she is?

6) Why is the story about Katie called "Futility"? What is futile here?

7) What does "Jerks" say about jock culture and male friendship?

8) In "Le Laurier Rose," the narrator judges a patron before learning she is an escaped murderer. What does this story say about perception and stereotypes?

9) How does "Newborn" blend the lines between reality and the supernatural?

10) How does "Now More Than Ever" portray capitalistic corporate culture, especially during the pandemic? Does the point of view affect the effectiveness of the message?

11) What does "Nunca Más" suggest about the gamification of language learning? (And how does this story echo themes in Edgar Allan Poe's "The Raven"?)

12) "Peach" shares a story about roommates. Can you relate to Anu's frustration with Peach? How could these two resolve their differences?

13) "Pillow Talk" shows the somewhat awkward morning after. What do you think of the narrator's conflicting feelings?

14) What is your reaction to "The Popular Virgin Blood Misconception"? How does this story play with expectations?

15) How does "Shitmix" compare to your own memories of first relationships?

16) How does the way "Starman" is told from the child's perspective affect your understanding of the story?

17) How well do you think "Texture" represents the current political climate?

18) What does "That Goddamn Cliché Pagliacci" say about the nature of humor and relief from suffering?

19) What do you think happened in "Tone Deaf"? Why is Giles so confused?

20) Why do you think it's called "Trinity"?

21) "Trypanophobia" is a fear of needles. What irrational fears do you have?

22) How does "White Rainbow 2028" view the future?

Author Bio

Cathleen Davies is a queer writer, teacher, and researcher, currently completing their PhD in Creative/Critical Writing at the University of East Anglia. They were born in the East Riding of Yorkshire, UK. They present seminars in high-schools, universities, and online, teaching a range of creative writing skills to people of all ages.

Davies also co-runs Aloka, an online journal for non-native and multilingual English speakers. Aloka strives to make the world of online literature as diverse as possible, amplifying underrepresented voices, and exploring the world through language, art, poetry, and translation.

Davies lives in Norwich, UK with their partner, two step kids and their 21-year-old cat, Fliss. In their spare time, they haunt their local music and poetry scene, drinking far too much beer.

You can find their other books: *Cheeky, Bloody Articles, And Marvel,* and *Fluid* at 4horsemenpublications.com, or on their website.

Discover more at
4HorsemenPublications.com

10% off using HORSEMEN10